ASK FOR ME TOMORROW

ASK FOR ME TOMORROW

HR Coursen

Copyright © 2000 by HR Coursen.

Library of Congress Number: 00-192026
ISBN #:　　　　Hardcover　　0-7388-3588-9
　　　　　　　Softcover　　　0-7388-3589-7

All rights reserved. No part of this book may be reproduced or transmitted in any form or by any means, electronic or mechanical, including photocopying, recording, or by any information storage and retrieval system, without permission in writing from the copyright owner.

This is a work of fiction. Names, characters, places and incidents either are the product of the author's imagination or are used fictitiously, and any resemblance to any actual persons, living or dead, events, or locales is entirely coincidental.

This book was printed in the United States of America.

To order additional copies of this book, contact:
Xlibris Corporation
1-888-7-XLIBRIS
www.Xlibris.com
Orders@Xlibris.com

CONTENTS

I. 7

II. 34

III. 95

IV. 137

Para J. R. Diaz-Fernandez, amigo y colegia

I.

Always, before a trip, I wish I were not going. I can remember, years ago, that I could hardly wait. But now I think of cancellations in strange and ugly cities, schedule changes, bad weather, jet lag. Old age creeps in on feline feet. The sense of adventure droops to detumescence.

    This trip, though, made me more apprehensive than usual. I knew that something was wrong. I knew that what Roger Baldwin had told me was wrong—incomplete at least, and incomplete enough to be dangerous to me. I was meant, it seemed, to stay within that zone of incompleteness, but how do you do that when there's that white space on the map waiting to be explored? Easy— you say, I'm no explorer! I was sure that I did not want to find out what that big picture was. The word sinister kept coming to mind. I do not give in to forebodings. They come, though, more often with time—I guess because time holds death within it, always closer than it was before—but to surrender to them is to yield to paralysis. I would do what I had been sent to do, file my report, get paid enough to last me for the rest of the year, and get back to the play I was working on. I would do what I had done so often in recent years—surrender to the rhythm of travel.

    The thump of overhead compartments, the whirring of compressors, the collecting of the empty champagne glasses and damp washcloths, the great weight of the aircraft straining along its slumped shoulders to overcome tons of inertia and lumber toward Newfoundland, the clunking of landing gear into place and the whine of flaps easing into airfoils gave me time to think about the past week. Usually, when I am finally in my seat in first class, I yield to the rhythms of travel. This time, though, I wished I had not climbed aboard Sabena 104 for Brussels, with a connecting flight to Sevilla. I could always book a flight back from Brussels. Sure, I thought. Even if I did not find out what any of this meant, I might still end up as Baldwin had—quite (and very prematurely) dead.

It had been a strange winter. I was anxious to escape from it. Montreal did not count. It had rained in Maine until the middle of January. All I had heard was the rain rattling outside on the gravel outside his window. That and the occasional zap as CMP decided to make us grateful for the times when we did have power by denying it to us periodically. Blue sky outages. It was a company that paid its executives exorbitantly, maintained a huge staff of public relations people, and believed that if you took a cord and bent it in half the electricity stopped flowing. January felt like November. That damp November of the soul of which Ishmael speaks had saturated me. Restlessness, boredom. The old fashioned winters—snow piled up so high at the intersections that you could not see the cars that could not see you—were gone forever. I had to go. Marie had been in New York for most of the time, but if she had been there, we would have been restless together. As it is, we'll be in Spain. Still, I had the strong feeling that I should stay right where I was. Some things are worse than boredom, though when you're bored it's hard to think of what they are.

I resisted briefly on the phone.

"Montreal is a dump."

"A dump." Baldwin repeated, as if wondering what the word meant.

"Cigarette smoke everywhere. The food is greatly overrated. And they don't want us foreigners there."

"Your French is pretty good."

"Even the waiters sneer when they think I'm not looking."

"I have reason to believe you want to come to Montreal."

"None that I can think of."

And more reasons than I could have known—that's what this story is all about—to keep me from making that short trip. I should have stayed in my rambling old house in the woods of Maine with my faithful dog, Casey, and my cantankerous computer—apparently the only one that had any trouble making it through the iron gates between 1999 and 2000. And besides, Marie—Roger's "reason to believe"—had been about to come here to visit me for a week, so Montreal was not on my list of sites to visit. And she was in New York on assignment for the month. Her assignment in Montreal had been in February, although I wondered how Roger had known even that much.

"Okay, but only if I stay at the Ritz Carleton."

"You have a room at the Queen Elizabeth."

And so, of course, I went to Montreal.

"Meet me at the Winston Churchill. Crescent Street. Cigar Lounge."

"No thanks. I get enough smoke without going to the source."

"All right. Bonaparte. Old Montreal. Two blocks from the waterfront. Eight."

We sat at a quiet table in the far corner of the dark dining room. It was a place framed for conspiracies, but I did not point out the sinister quality of the shadows to Roger Baldwin. He was all business.

"Larry, your task is simple."

"Okay. I'll need a photographer."

"Anyone in mind?"

"Maybe."

"Well, she should keep you out of trouble."

This little bit of sparring was about Marie, of course. She was damned good with a camera, and she'd been after me to take her somewhere out of the grim northeast all winter long. Since she had been in New York and had been coming up to see me for a couple of days in Maine—the couple of days I was here in Canada—this trip would placate her. I did want to placate her. The thought of any day without her voice, the thought of any moment when I did not anticipate seeing her was, yes, unthinkable. More unthinkable thoughts were rousing themselves at the threshold of each day I did not see her.

"And it's not your money, is it, Roger."

"Your expenses will continue to be paid until you turn in your report. Your check will be cut immediately."

"And all you want me to do is to report about what happens to the bulls?"

"Precisely. Your little piece of the larger picture will be invaluable. Anti-bullfighting associations already exist. There's one in Holland, for example, so what you give us will be invaluable."

"To whom?"

"There's a larger picture here, Larry. Anything that gets in the way of unfettered trade—and that includes working conditions, worker's wages, abuse of women, abuse of animals has got to be chronicled. What we do, in going into detail, is to show that we have looked at the issues. We then say we are resolved to solve them. What you don't understand is how powerful the animal protection lobby is. These aren't just the people who say we have to let bears forage in our backyards. We are talking big bucks. Unless we show that we are working in directions they approve, they pour a lot of money in against us. Money and rhetoric. What we are spending on this is small potatoes compared to what we'd spend to fight them. Understand?"

"I understand small potatoes. I'm from Maine."

He was telling me, of course, that I didn't understand these things. They were for adults. Did I hear a little gloating in his voice? I had known him for years and had done some work for him when he had styled himself a Broadway producer. He paid well—when it was someone else's money—and it was easy enough to do the kind of research he wanted. People who don't do that sort of thing have a great aversion to libraries, microfilm, and search engines. They think of it all as some sort of mystery that requires secret knowledge. It does, of course. Like almost any other craft or skill, it demands that you know what to seek, what to ask for, and how to recognize it when it turns up. Well, that's the secret of life, isn't it? I resented Baldwin's ability to change my life with the snap of a finger. But, then, his voice had always had that finger snap quality—as it to say, this is a one-time offer, not to be repeated.

"You make it seem very plausible."

Clearly, The Planetary Organization of Finance, or its subsidiary organization, Globe Land: Organization and Plans, didn't give a damn about protecting animals, but they had to look as if they did. I tried to think, well, it's their money, but I hated to be enlisted in something as phony as this seemed to be. Still, however, Roger was hardly letting me in on what was really happening. I was part of an infinite regress of mirrors, each one showing the same image in an increasingly smaller perspective, each one concealing some truth that lay down there beneath the surface that was deeper than never.

"Let me just fill in a bit more of the picture for you."

He said all of this with the patience of an over-worked teacher of seventh grade dealing with one of her slower pupils.

"You've heard of bioengineered animals."

It was a statement, so I nodded.

"Cloning," I said.

"That's the obvious example. What we mean by the term is the borrowing of genes from one animal and implanting them in another. Pigs can be made to produce feces that contain less phosphorus than usual and thus are less harmful to the environment."

"And no doubt made to smell like Chanel."

He ignored my amusing comment and went on with his lecture.

"But take a genetically altered salmon. It could grow bigger, faster, and taste just as good as anything from the cold lochs of Scotland, but, if it got out somehow, and mated with wild fish, it could kill off the species. Environmental disruptions have already occurred, like the invasion of zebra mussels in the Hudson River."

"Zebra mussels. I don't see where the bulls fit in."

He had lost his patience long ago. Now, he demonstrated that loss.

"You don't have to. This is a mosaic of such grand design, that. . . . all you have to do is collect the data—particularly descriptions—back it up with photos—good ones, I agree—and you can be back to work in two weeks."

I did need the money. Bullies work on real fears. But Roger did not want to admit to himself that he was a bully. He calmed himself down and decided to explain something to me. I could see the effort at patience in the angry set of his mouth.

He waved a newspaper in front of me.

"See this op-ed piece?"

"So?"

"See what a smokescreen it is?"

"I suppose."

"Tell me, then."

I knew what he wanted, of course. I had to understand the dynamics before he could trust me to do anything intelligent. It was always a test. You never passed it.

Okay. The editorial equates the goals of the so-called leftists who are opposing the Globe Land: Organization and Plans agenda to those of the far right. The mistrust of technology, internationalism, emphasis on outmoded traditions, fear of supergovernmental controls, suspicion of electoral politics could be an agenda of the far right.

"So what? Plenty of far right people were protesting too."

"We know that. Most people don't. They see the same unwashed kids out there who shouted 'Hell no, we won't go' in the 60s."

"Okay. I get the point."

"Which is?"

"That you smear the left in the interest of the corporations."

"That's roughly it."

"That's exactly it. But that's only the surface.

"Of course. If you read the op-ed pieces in the *New York Times* or the *Washington Post* you are getting the sophisticated surface."

"And you want me to go to Spain to contribute to the surface?"

Now he was getting exasperated. He knew I'd go. He knew I was giving him a hard time. He was also one of those people who moved too fast through the preliminaries of any negotiation—as if he alone had that big picture in his head.

"Look, Larry, it's an assignment. It will fill in part of the pattern. I am telling you all of this because you are a friend."

What he was saying, of course, is that he could drag someone off the street to do this job. With friends like Roger . . .

"It will fill in part of the surface that hides the real goal of all this research," I said.

"That's a cynical way to look at it."

"Sure. And an accurate way. I am working for you, don't forget."

"I don't. Not for a minute. You are just a fragment of one aspect of the research. Animal rights and their violation worldwide. Spain and bullfighting are a dramatic instance. Larger components are workers rights, human rights and poverty, human rights and disease, and the environment, including wild life, of course. This is going to do some good."

"For someone, no doubt, but not the people it's intended to help."

He said nothing.

"So I am one per cent of ten percent."

"Don't overestimate yourself. You are hardly a fraction of that."

"And all this frantic research permits GLOP to go their merry way."

"Ultimately heavily conditioned by what all this research turns up."

"I doubt that, Roger. Are you kidding your other people into believing that they are accomplishing something? The big guys are paying a bundle to fund all this diversion. They are also paying experts to prove that pollution is a thing of the past—you can see the sky line of LA again!—and that global warming is a fabricated scare tactic, or that it is changing the climate for the better, and, oh yeah, and that second hand smoke is benign. Pretty soon, reputable studies will be saying that the earth is flat."

Roger was at the end of a short rope.

"I don't have to ask you why I chose you for this one."

"Let's not get into that."

"How well do you know the bulls?"

"I'll do some reading."

"What does that mean?"

"What it means, dammit. I'll become an instant expert"

"How's your Spanish."

"Okay."

"What does that mean?"

"It means that it will take me a half hour. A lot of it is in gesture and in the eyes. It's not the same in Andalucia."

"What's different?"

"The eyes."

His own eyes were shifting toward something else, something that did not include me.

"If you had any doubts, Roger..."

"I know, I know. You've accepted the assignment."

He handed me a half-sheet of paper.

"Here's where you deliver the report."

It looked like a simple job—and I needed the money.

As I came around to the hallway from the elevators on the 10th floor, I saw activity at the end of the hall near Roger Baldwin's room. Yellow tape was strung from one wall to the other. Clearly I would not be able to stroll past the yellow tape and the uniformed policeman who stood in front of it. I could have identified myself as a business associate, but that would mean all kinds of questions and delays, along with the prospect of being identified by whoever had knocked Roger off. I was convinced that that was what had happened. Sometimes you know. It is like looking at a photograph in the newspaper. You know that it's a picture of someone who has just died. I took the elevator down to nine and came up one flight to the emergency exit. I pushed the door open carefully until I could see Roger's door.

Two men in civilian suits were conferring in the hallway.

"We can move it?"

"Crime scene says we can."

"Right. Secure an elevator."

"Sir, all elevators exit at the lobby."

"We'll take the body to the second floor and down the steps to the basement from there. We'll meet the coroner at the delivery ramp."

The other man made a call on his cell phone.

"He'll be there."

"Let's wrap it up, then. Tell the hotel they can begin cleaning the room."

The hotel will vacuum the room, then move the bed over that nasty stain in the rug.

"Yes, sir," I thought, "We happen to have a last minute cancellation. A pleasant room looking out on the Rue de Universite. I'll check to see whether it has been made up yet."

Timing is everything.

I pulled the door closed very slowly again, but it made a "clunk." I skipped up to the 11th floor landing as soundlessly as I could and slipped into the hallway just as the door below me opened.

I had not unpacked, so I had only to slip my shaving kit and a plastic bag of dirty laundry into my suitcase and I could be off. But where to? I'd take the late flight to Cincinnati and then back to Portland. The long way, but Air Nova wasn't going to Portland until eleven a.m. tomorrow.

I noticed the light on my phone blinking.

"You have one message."

"'Meet me at Kam Fung on Clark at eight.'"

I needed no name to go with the voice. It seems that Olivia Baldwin had come up to join Roger for a vacation after his business dealings were completed. They were probably flying from here to some warmer place. That had been the plan. I listened to the tape again, this time for aesthetic reasons. The voice summoned an old urgency.

I stood beside my suitcase for a moment and looked down the long avenue toward Mount Royal. It was a bleak perspective here in this northernmost of large cities—lights glaring on wet black streets, snow rutted in the gutters, a sense of wind riding down from the grim buildings of McGill, picking up crystals of cold and chunks of dampness as it came.

It was almost eight.

"You know where Kam Fung is? On Clark?"

"1008," he said in French. I hoped he was naming the address, not the fare.

I swung my bag in the back seat and climbed in after it.

Olivia Baldwin—she had been Olivia Babcock of the Long Island Babcocks—had one of those faces you saw in a Busby Berkeley musical from years ago, where each member of the chorus pauses for a moment in front of the camera and you want to say, "Wait! Wait! That girl! What's her name?" But the faces move past and they are all staring at the lids of their coffins by now. Olivia's had moved past me—to Baldwin. I still recalled the party at Sutton Place. It was early spring, so the windows were open. The season drifted in via the East River—it was the murky New York smell, the scents of drifting garbage, of wool, silk, Chanel, of crisp voices and calculation, of musk oiling in pores and the scratchy lisp of sexuality in some of the voices. Baldwin at the time was on some desperate edge or other—like that poor bastard on the ledge, everyone below shouting "Jump! Jump!" Baldwin was far from the confident bastard he would be a few years later, but he had persuaded Olivia that she should join him and by the time I got back to her side with another glass of wine, it was done. That was New York, of course. It had happened before. Usually, I got a brief frightened glance and then the story. You want me to do anything about it? I'd ask. No, I'm just glad you're here. I'm fine now. Olivia, though, had looked at me coolly as if I had completed my mission by handing her the chablis. Was it important enough for me to drop everything and fight for her? No. I was at the party to meet a backer for one of my plays, and Olivia was here because I was. I think she thought I'd raise a fuss about Roger's trying to pick her up.

I did ask her once, a year or so later, just out of curiosity. She was beautiful and I could sense a bit of intellectual regret when I saw her again, as I did often enough in those days. I was curious about how a man—even one as persuasive as Roger Baldwin had been—could win a woman like Olivia while I was at the bar.

"What did he tell you?"

"I have forgotten the details."

"Was it about money?"

"That was certainly one of my weaknesses. I had no money. Roger didn't then, either, but he came from money and looked it."

"So did you, and so did you."

"I had had that fight with Daddy."

"Love then," I said with just the touch of a sneer.

I had not told Olivia that I loved her. Perhaps Roger had.

"Not then."

"Adventure."

"That was it. It was tone, not destination."

Yes, Roger had been a master of tone. He had translated his own fear into excitement and taken her along for the ride. The real reason, though, must have been that I did not care enough. If that sounds self-serving, so be it. My own lack of massive emotional investment certainly saved me from a nasty crash-and-burn when she was gone. Fortunately, I had met Marie, who had showed up to take some photos of the rehearsal of a play that barely lasted until the photos were published in the *Observer*. Now that *was* a difficult time for me—the closing of a play—but Marie had been the kind of miracle that suddenly gleams into view when you cannot otherwise think of anything good.

Roger had known about Olivia and me, of course, and had resented the relationship we'd had—always thinking (I think) that it had something that his relationship with her had not had. Well, ours had had sex. Roger was one of those men who wanted all their women to be virgins. What he had gotten—the bastard—was love. Olivia had found something in him that he had been unable to discover himself.

She had made the reservations in my name.

I checked my bag and my raincoat and looked for her.

And there she was, out across the fragrant steam of a dining room in which the light seemed to flare and fade between where I stood and the table in the corner where she sat. She was not anxiously staring at the door, but glancing at the menu as if it were a cast of characters awaiting its play. Her light blonde hair—the kind that will turn to gray without anyone noticing it—framed her gray eyes as they looked up from the huge orange and black menu. The eyes were the color of a lake I used to go to in New Hampshire, just as the sun went under a cloud. She lifted her eyebrows to let me know she saw me coming across the dining room to her.

"No one knows I'm here. Roger did, of course."

"I am sorry."

"I'm booked at the Ritz Carlton. A suite. He was going to meet me."

I said I was sorry again.

"They said it was suicide."

We looked at each other for a moment. Whatever it had been, it had not be a self-inflicted wound.

"You didn't . . . ?"

"No. I didn't go near the place.—look this is dangerous, Larry."

"Clearly. What's it all about?"

"I have been too scared to react yet. But there's something about the abuse of animals that . . . It's not just Bob Barker, J. Ron Hubbard's money, and Animalove. There's more to it than that."

"I'm sure there is, Livy, but I am going to file my report and get my check. I am going to come out foursquare against the killing of dogs to test insulin. Let people die. I am going to say that Bodyshop's refusal to use animals in its product experiments is the greatest step in social progress since the abolition of child labor."

I watched her fear work at the sides of her mouth. Or, perhaps, that was the beginning of grief.

"I don't think you'll be able to."

"Why not?"

"Oh, they'll let you look at whatever you are supposed to look at, but that's not all there is, and once you begin to look further . . ."

"At what?"

"I don't know."

"Do you have any ideas?"

"Yes, but only speculation. And it is dangerous to speculate."

"Clearly."

"Roger knew something."

"Something that you don't know."

"Yes."

"Any papers?"

"There were some. In his office at home."

"What?"

"I did peek. I admit it. That is why I am so scared. But they don't make sense."

"Like what?"

"Things like POOF wants strong report on abuse of animals."

"So? That's what I am supposedly working on."

"That's just an example. Things like Encourage Protesters. Fund Anti Missile System Support. Just quick notes. Not even complete sentences sometimes."

"Like that one."

"Subject to be inferred, you bastard. Always a verb in their memos. Action."

"Shoot to kill. Sorry! These were Roger's memos?"

"No. These snippets were on a paper labeled Policy Positions. And they were in the POOF folder."

"Like this?"

I took the memo Roger had given me from my jacket pocket.

"Exactly."

"So—we are not asking what POOF has to do with the abuse of animals question. Roger's explanation made some sense. But the old Starwars Program, Reagan's nitwit scheme—if that is what that means?—or protests? Protests against POOF?"

"You see?," she said, pouring herself some rice wine.

I didn't see, except that it was dangerous. Those memos had killed Roger Baldwin. I understood what she meant. How did I look at one issue without finding out more than I wanted to find out—even if I tried to be blind?

"Look, Livy"—I had not called her Livy for a few years now, but the name came naturally to my tongue—"I have my bag checked. I am on my way—somewhere. Then to Sevilla."

I pointed at the empty bottle of Tsingtao beside my empty glass as the waiter drifted up.

"Another please."

"It's too late to get a flight."

"I'm booked on one to Cincinnati. And there's a late one to Boston."

She did not want to be alone tonight, but was much too much of a lady to say so.

I could see that she was frightened, and that grief had yet to come. I think she still expected to meet Roger later that night, or early the next morning.

I put the issue aside for a moment, while I flicked my chopsticks through bits of squab marinated in some white liquor. I was hungry. Death on the 10th floor, my escape from the hotel, whether from danger to me or merely because of my built-in paranoia, Livy's sudden appearance—these factors had not defeated my hunger. Perhaps they had encouraged it.

"Look, if they can purchase a finding of suicide," I began, orchestrating my insight with the chopsticks.

She, too, was hungry, mincing shrimp to her wide mouth—the only assymetrical thing about her—with quick thrusts.

"It means they are too big to fool around with," she said, completing my thought.

"So I don't intend to fool around, Livy."

"Just write your little report?"

"Not little to me. I'll still get paid."

"I know. Fifty thousand."

"Plus expenses."

"I won't ask you whether it's worth it, Larry, but don't you see?"

"What?"

She looked around the restaurant. No one was near us, but our low murmur—had anyone been listening—would have been an undertone to the crowlike chatter that punctuated the wafting flavors of the room. We could have been in Shanghai—two whites against a background of yellow.

"I don't know exactly. Roger was aiming you at something. It wasn't just the report."

I liked her metaphor. Yes, I was like the man in the cannon, but no one had figured out the trajectory, or the target. I would be exploded outward to who knew where? To a hard landing. It would be like Roger Baldwin. He was a deal-maker. He'd try to put together ten or a dozen, trading on New Haven connections and his father's tailor, and then he'd become one of the string-pullers for Global Liaison Organizational Programs—good old GLOP—and all of his deals went through. One had killed him. It could kill me.

"It's late," I said. "We are both tired. In shock."

"It's later than it's ever been."

"I think that I am in danger of over-reacting."

I cracked open my fortune cookie.

It did not tell me how wise I was, how happy in my friends, or proffer long life to me. It was empty.

Livy stared at its two tiny confectionary caves.

"No," I said. "I just don't eat it. Never eat a fortune cookie that doesn't give you a good fortune."

"That one gave you none at all."

I shrugged and put a credit card down on top of the bill.

"Does this mean you are coming back to the Ritz with me?"

I wanted to ask—does *what* mean? An empty fortune cookie? I glanced at my watch.

"Yes," I said.

"Let's take separate cabs," she said." I feel eyes everywhere."

And so to Sherbrooke Street, a suite filled with antique furniture, with a marble bathroom and all kinds of amenities for me to shove into my shaving kit. I got to stay at the Ritz after all.

"Cancelled. That stinks!"

"Sir, if you do not stop, I shall be forced to call airport security."

"Your job is to get me and these people to Portland, Maine. I hope you and your airline rot in the hottest part of hell."

"I shall be forced to call airport security."

"Well, they'd put me up, wouldn't they? You bastards are costing me another expensive night in this fleabag town."

It was one thing for the Sunday flight to have been cancelled. It had snowed the night before. I remember awakening to the pillowy sound of snow against the windows. I slid from the bed and looked down at the stark lights on the icy white street. Nothing moved except the wind. I knew then that it would be no use even trying to get to the airport that day.

We rebooked the suite. Certainly no one was coming in that day and the hotel was happy to have us. We learned that the city, in its wisdom, had let its maintenance contract expire as of 31 March. This was the first of April.

"April Fools! as we used to say. Theses Frenchmen are stupider than I thought."

"That's pretty stupid!" she said. "And they are French Canadians."

"They like to be thought of as French, except when they feel they are being victimized. Then they become members of an oppressed post-colonial society."

"The world is full of victims."

"Some of it is attitude," I said.

We were finishing our coffee.

"You don't think we should try to get to the airport?"

"Assuming we get there, it will be a madhouse. We can't get though on the phone either. And what would they tell us? We'll go out the first thing tomorrow. Maybe the runways will have melted off enough for them to operate the airplanes."

"No shops will be open."

"Trapped on Sherbrooke Street on a Sunday."

"I called last night—just after I called you—and made arrangements for Roger—for Roger's body—to be sent to New York. I called his older sister. She's going to get the family minister in Rye and set up the funeral—memorial service—there."

She looked down at the cream twisting like a galaxy in her coffee cup.

"Thank heavens!"

"No newspapers," I said.

"Newpapers?"

"I meant the Sunday *New York Times*."

"So?"

"Let's hang out in the suite. Run room service ragged. Sample the wine list. I'll book a limo to the airport for tomorrow morning. I just have to call Maine."

"Maine?"

"About my dog. I left my dog there."

That was true, but it was also a lie.

"I have to tell Marie that I will be a day late," I said.

Livy nodded, and said nothing. Hell, she'd been married in the mean time!

I could see the wind out there, picking up the dampness from the snow and flinging it at the few persons bending along the avenue. If it had to be winter, I wanted to work my way through it at home. Still, being alone on this day would have been intolerable, and I guessed it would have been worse for Livy Baldwin.

The airport was chaos on Monday, too. It was one rung of Dante's trilogy—where they send the ex-smokers, to pay for their stupidity, to be among the current smokers.

I got Livy on her plane to New York. She had a first class ticket, so that was easy. I felt sorry for the steerage people and their infants. Two planeloads of passengers sat in and around the plastic chairs of the waiting room. Many would wait all day, then be thrust back through customs to seek a room in that grim and foreign city.

"Keep your chin up, Livy. Just do what they tell you to do for a couple of days. I'm glad Roger's family is taking over."

"So am I. You helped, Larry."

Perhaps I had. I had taken her feet off the rug and maybe her mind off of things like conspiracy, death, the lonely times just outside the door.

"You're the one who has to be careful," she said, bringing her body close and kissing me goodbye.

My loins felt drained, like an hourglass at the end of its hour, but it was a good feeling, as if the grains of that particular time should have crossed into the drift and spun through light to drop as softly as that snowstorm into oblivion below.

I knew I was tired when I started to get metaphysical.

And then, of course, Air Canada—specifically Air Nova—cancelled the short hop to Portland, Maine. It was only a sixteen passenger plane, but they had more fannies that wanted to go somewhere else, so the plane encountered mechanical difficulties.

"We have no cars that can go into the United States at this hour."

"How about Buffalo?"

I could get a car to Toronto. I could get one to Ottawa. I took a risk, though, if I drove a car with a Canadian destination to Maine. I would if I had to.

"We can give you a full-sized car to Buffalo."

"Buffalo, then."

By this time, of course, I had been talking to myself for several hours.

"Okay. Pick up 28 to 10. Toward Sherbrooke. Pick up signs for 89. Let's get the hell out of here."

The map showed Route 89 just at the bottom, a number, not even the beginning of a road. For French Canada the world does not exist below its borders. Do they believe the world is flat? Certainly the drive south to find 89 was flat and, to my New England eyes, dull and ugly. It was a relief to reach customs.

"No. I didn't buy a thing."

"No Cuban cigars?"

"Sorry. I'd give you one if I had."

"And I'd accept!"

I was happy to roll past the upland farms of Vermont, still shrouded in snow that glinted in the late afternoon and then to watch the last sun touch the mountains of New Hampshire. It felt like home. As soon as the sun went down, though, loneliness settled in. The pines were etched against the gray light. The single island along a narrow stretch of lake was alone and the houses glowed luminously as if only television sets were inside. The sun had outlined the homes on the far side of the road, and the mountains of New Hampshire had risen like clouds across the trees. But now it was cold. I toked in some heat.

I also felt that someone was coming after me. That body rolling out of that room, the corpse that had grown four metal legs with wheels on them in its final evolutionary feat in Montreal had been very dead, more dead because I had known it when it was alive, when irony and intelligence lit the eyes of it and curled the mouth of it. Now the eyes were rotting and the mouth was stiff, probably sewn shut over that cynical smile and teeth that would need no more work. A good thing about death—no more trips to the dentist.

Alone, however, tired, in a big iron from Hertz at twilight, I was sure someone was following me. If lights stayed on too long behind me, I slowed. If they slowed . . . I breathed again when they turned off.

"This car was due in Bangor at two this afternoon."

"It was in Montreal at three. Same time zone."

"I can't accept this car."

"It's all yours. Slot number 17."

I put the keys down and walked away. My own car was parked at Thrifty. I expected a "Sir! Sir!" from the woman at the Hertz desk, but my glance back found her staring at the yellow invoice.

Home again—I did not want to leave again in a few days.

Casey had been delighted to see me again, of course, but I think the only person he really missed was my daughter, Katherine—no one called her Kate or, heaven forbid, Katy—who had not been here in over a year. Almost two years now. Casey held an occasional plaintive look under his setter's smile. Happy as I am to see you—isn't *she* with you this time? He adjusted easily enough to my neighbor, who had dogs of his own, and to Marie, when she came.

I walked down to my mail box and was opening it, when a car came over the rise going much too fast. Casey, who had come along with me to check the mail, growled. I was about to turn and motion the idiot to slow down when I saw the car veer toward me. I jumped into the space between the mail boxes and watched the bumper of the car miss the post on which my mail box stood by a couple of inches. It was an old Chrysler, blue paint faded by the sun and spotted by the acne of rust. Its driver wore a plaid shirt with a baseball cap pulled down near his eyes. It was a he. The plates were Maine, with its dead lobster steaming on the back. I did not get the number. Casey gave two sharp, angry barks in the direction of the disappearing junker.

So—what was that? I thought, reaching into the post box and automatically pulling catalogues, a Central Maine Power bill, dunning me for last month's outages, and some letters from the metal shadows.

In Maine, perhaps more than in other states, there's a real line between the natives and people like me—"from away." We have money, diplomas from expensive schools and colleges, fancy cars, and homes in Florida for when the winter winds become too strong. They have minimum wage, or dig clams, drive junkers that end up rusting in the weeds with fading "For Sale" signs on them and ancient inspection stickers on the windshields, and resentment. One of them seeing a yuppie in his Brooks Brothers shirt at a mail box full of dividend checks decided to give the son-of-a-bitch a scare.

If it were only that . . .

I walked back up the driveway, looking at the last grin of an icy tireprint, listening to the moisture of the storm of a few days ago percolating into the ground and running down the veins of relaxing frost. I had chosen to live in a red-neck state whose primary newspaper had never come out against the war in Vietnam but had just let the matter drift out over its subscription list. That was my choice. But if that old Chrysler had been a cleverly disguised warning, I resented it. We had allowed the enemy to invade us without resistance.

The guy had been wearing a black cap, possibly a Yankees cap. If so, it was a nice touch—a raising of a middle-finger at the Red Sox fans who forlornly eke out their lives in the hills and valleys, on the coastline. Raiders sweatshirts did not make such a complex statement. They just said, I am a nihilist, even if I don't know what the word means. Casey was independent enough not to accompany me all the way back to the house. There were squirrels in those woods.

"Anything?" Marie asked as I came up the steps and into the house.

"No," I said.

"What's all that?"

"Let's see."

Here was a note from Baldwin! Had I made some sort of grisy

mistake in Montreal. Was he still alive? I had made all those assumptions! Did Livy know?

"What's wrong?"

I looked at the postmark. Montreal. The day he had been killed. The day after I had seen him.

"Nothing," I said. "Instructions."

From a dead man.

"You look, as they say, as if you had seen a ghost."

I was reading his words, but I was not a young prince being asked to revenge a father's murder.

"You will pose as an aficionado of the bulls. You say your Spanish is 'good enough' . . ."

"It is, you bastard."

"That's known as apostrophe."

"What?"

"Speaking to something absent or inanimate, as if it could reply."

"You're right. It's from Baldwin."

"Is he—from Baldwin?"

"Before he was killed."

I read her a paragraph.

"Although I am reluctant, I authorize you to take Marie as your photographer. I know *her* skills are good enough. I suggest that, although you may wish to travel together, you make separate arrangements in Sevilla. I have booked her at the Inglaterra."

"Typical Baldwin. He expresses his reluctance, then gives in. A guilt trip."

"He won't collect on it."

"Don't make a bet. Notice, he's made the arrangements for us, having suggested it."

"You sure you want me to go?"

"No. I want you to stay here and stare at the trees growing leaves. It isn't Roger's prudery speaking there. He thinks there's some danger involved."

"He thinks right, I guess. Past tense."

"If I thought there was danger . . ."

I did not tell her of my brush with the old Chrysler. There was danger!

"Maybe there is danger," I said. "Let's just be careful."

"You are born and you take your chances. I think I'll take a walk."

"I'll come with you."

"You want to take a walk?"

"Yeah. I got out of shape on that damned trip."

"Three days?"

"I dragged in a lot of second-hand smoke."

"They say it can do no harm."

"And I'll bet I can find a people within a ten mile radius who believe that God made the world out of unpopped pop corn."

She was baiting me, probably because she liked to walk alone—with Casey—but I thought that old car might still be rattling around the area. The road he had come down was one-way to the ocean.

"So what did you do on the extra day—Sunday?"

She probably knew, and was punishing me for coming on this walk with her.

"Drank."

That was true.

"In the company of a beautiful woman, of course," I said.

That was also true.

She gave me one of those "I don't know whether I should take the time to be angry at this asshole or not" looks and let it go. She looked at me again as if she believed me. I had a sudden, terrible feeling that it did not matter to her, that is, that I did not matter to her. I had to hold myself very still and say nothing.

I had met Marie at the National Gallery in London in the French Impressionists section. She looked very French—dark eyes, dark hair, a beret and silk scarf—so I said something to her in what I assumed to be her native tongue.

"You're fortunate that I am not French," she said, in English.

"I know I am," I said.

It was one of those afternoons that Hollywood filmmakers would have chosen to begin a film. Nelson would have surveyed Trafalgar Square and the inevitably unnecessary caption would have appeared. "London."

"I know a great Italian restaurant," I said.

"You must really be a linguist!"

"Ah ha! New York!"

"Long Island."

"Garden City."

"What street?"

The Paradiso e Inferno was right across the road from where I was staying, The Savoy.

I had read Marie accurately in one sense. She was a student. She wasn't starving, but she was willing to be treated to the savory, many-coursed, sauce and garlic-heavy steamy cuisine of Southern Italy, absorbed with crusty bread and pursued down the throat with two carafes of the house red wine. We were on the balcony, on the same level as the kitchen, overlooking the dining room with its windows on the Strand. We had the balcony to ourselves, so it was as if we were in a quiet zone of our own, overhearing a festival going on somewhere else, getting all of the benefits—including the rise of flavors from the center of meat and from the surface of exotic condiments—but none of the crowded disadvantages. I had thought I was just a few years beyond the enjoyment of that precise kind of isolation. Marie was not averse to coming across the road to see what the rooms at the Savoy were like. My room, at least.

She had just finished studying photography with Benjamin at the Portman Square Conservatory, so we flew back to New York together. Getting her upgraded on Virgin Atlantic turned out to be on the right side of possible, so I did not have to trail back through the plane to visit her. She napped below my shoulder, her seat full back, while I read, and the plane defeated time in the direction of home. Time is always defeated in that direction.

My own failure in London—to get Richard Eyre to produce a play of mine that he had read and liked ("Would break the budget, old boy. Sorry!")—was absorbed in this new beginning. We had both known at some point when we looked at each other through the steam between us at Paradiso e Inferno that this was going to be a good wave to ride. That had been five years ago. I had just broken up with Livy—or she with me—and, while I told myself that I savored my freedom, I realized a few minutes after I met Marie how lonely I had been.

That night with Livy at the Ritz in Montreal I had gotten rid of something that otherwise would have nagged at me. Livy was free again! That would have shadowed the edges of my relationship with Marie. Some men cannot make a commitment. I was one of them. The good thing about my infidelity—if that is what it was—in Montreal is that I proved to myself that all Livy and I had was the sex. Very good—but not self-sustaining at 43 as it would have been at 20. And she knew it too. We had parted with some sadness but no regret.

Marie did not need the validation of relationship. That frightens me and keeps me from asking for any commitment from her. She might say no. And, if I invited that fragile moment into being, everything might shatter. It was like watching a glass blower at work.

She has her inner laughter, and sometimes she shares the cause of laughter with others, with me. I want that to continue.

I pointed at a stump, now black and rotted and partly filled with a pool of melted snow.

"That's where that old elm used to be," I said, as we turned down the dirtroad.

"Thinking of Katherine."

I hadn't been, consciously, but yes, I had been thinking of my daughter, who had not been in contact for a couple of years now.

We were estranged, as the saying goes. How do you explain divorce to a twelve year old? How do you explain marriage to yourself? Katherine—not Kate, and certainly not Katy—was—what?—22 now. I had rejected *her*, of course, when she had been twelve, not her mother. A father can do nothing for his daughters except hope, and the hopes turn around a father's conventional images—much different than those of a man's—and a daughter is wise not to fit the father's perceived patterning. But that wisdom leads to estrangement.

"Sure a lot of her in your play."

"Yes, and I am conscious of that."

"You are?"

"A writer is conscious of almost everything he—or she does. People think we create out of some unconscious urge. Not so. Writing is a craft. We think."

"You think it's a craft?"

"I know it's a craft."

"You should have a dog."

"I did think of that, believe it or not, but two things. Iphigenia did not have a dog and you don't bring a dog on stage."

"Unless you are Shakespeare."

"Very early in his career. I think he saw how the damned dog stole the show."

What Marie was getting at, of course, was that we could tell that Casey missed Katherine. Casey's smile—and he did smile!—betrayed a certain sadness at times, and the alacrity with which he got up when he heard a car before any human ears could detect its coming diminished quickly when he realized that it wasn't Katherine in that car.

I moved to Marie's right and edged her to the side of the road.

The agitation of gravel below the hill argued the coming of a car.

"They can see us!"

"That's the problem."

We waved at neighbors who lived on the point overlooking Maquoit Bay.

"You are jumpy."

"I think we should go separately. We'll come back together."

"To Spain? Okay. You are spooked, but you're the boss. I do want you to visit now and then at the Inglaterra."

"I plan to do that. I hope you will visit at the Alfonso Trece as well."

I live on a dirt road off a narrow, patched and pot-holed macadam road. I have always prized the isolation. Just trees, wind, power outages, candles and a generator, and occasionally a distant dog barking across the crusted snow. That night, for the first time, I locked the doors. As it turned out, we came back separately as well.

II.

I was the only non-European on the plane from Brussels to Sevilla, apparently, so my luggage came to its own separate carousel. A single customs agent looked at my bag.

"Ropas?"

"Si, y un navaje de afietar."

Clothes and a razor.

"Bueno."

He stamped my passport.

I stood for a moment in the shadows outside the terminal. It was not yet tropical summer in Sevilla, but I could feel heat riding the hydrocarbons of the entrance to the airport and sense the August that would turn the palm-fronds yellow and change the Guadalquivir into a silver ingot at noon. I still had a trace of the sleety chill of Montreal quivering above my elbows, but the warmth did not dispel my sense of being followed and watched.

"Senor Kane?"

"Si."

"Me llamo Miguel. I take you to su hotel."

I blinked in the light folding in under the canopy. I had been reading—history, terminology—"mocho," "mogon," "molinete"—and I had absorbed what I needed for the pose of expert. Writers can do that—they have to in order to suggest the knowledge that goes into their fictions. I know that other people resent that absorbency, but it's what writers have to do before they write. I could handle the scene if I uttered only the occasional word—"sardo," "sartenazo," "semental"—but other things awaited me here, sinister things. The word was "sinister." I could not get it out of my head, and I was already doubtful that I could handle it. Tengo miedo. I am afraid.

I began to feel better, though, as I wandered the closed-in streets of the old quarter, designed so that, assuming an enemy got it, he'd never find his way out again. The ghosts of the Moors sang in every small plaza of Sevilla. In the water, moving up in fountains, a constant, soothing background along the stones of the tiny lanes and alleys of the city. The Moors, having learned how to move water into arid climates, also learned to cast the spell of its serenity.

The larger avenues were warm, riding spring like an incoming tide past the palm and orange trees. The horses were decked, manes and tails, with interwoven braids—red and white, or green and white, the colors of Andalucia. As a pair clopped along in front of a carriage, their four legs became two for an instant as they passed, so perfect was their shared rhythm.

I wandered toward the river and sat on a bench in the sun. The tourist boat, La Luna de Sevilla, waited to slide down the Guadalquivir. Its loudspeaker played Elgar, to make people move slowly toward the gangplank. My own head moved out with a luminosity that I could almost feel. I saw phantom ceremonies, me and others moving toward some unseen place in time to the never-tiring orchestra. Why had I insisted that Marie take a separate flight? She'd know what to do about my jetlag.

I gazed up the river at the 1920s bridge across to Triana, a construction of linked cantilevers, with steel circles inside, each circle smaller as the arch leans up into the thoroughfare. The art deco contrasted with the wings of the newer bridge built for Expo '92. The latter threatened to take off and disappear during the next windstorm. The bridge to Triana held its gravity close to the river, now shading with silver as the sun slids like a gong into the sea.

La Luna de Sevilla slowly glides the green Guadalquivir, where the ocean's edge, the bridges and the big ships, the anchorage of Columbus and conquistadors, rides the molten glint of afternoon. Across from the lazy boat are the orange trees and tiles of Triana, a calm evening easing into stars, the toss and glide of birds that wheel the gold spaces and quiver on the aerials, sending signals down of wings pausing, traces of feathery design, a ghost ascending of moon through the blue distance, a sliver through silver clouds, along the olive river.

I was being watched, but I could feel no threat. That was it. Whoever it was was just watching. There was nothing I could do that would provoke any active response from them, so I will do nothing. Let them watch me wander around aimlessly.

I was supposed to stay up for the duration of the day—or so I had read—but I could barely put a foot forward. It was time to collect my key and, if I had the energy, kick from my shoes and pull the covers down. I might, I thought, just sleep on top of the covers. At least I think that is what I was thinking. I did get my shoes off.

I was there in time to pick Marie up the next morning. I would not have been had Miguel not called my room, telling me he had the car waiting.

I was still haggard, as if I had been travelling all night—I guess I had been, the motion still wheeling away in my inner ear even as I dreamed of perpetual motion—but she was at once cool and bright-eyed.

"Good trip?"

"I like those big seats. I had a drink and dinner and next thing I knew I smelled the coffee brewing."

"I can't sleep on airplanes."

"You snore."

"And that's why I can't sleep on airplanes?"

Miguel held he door open for Marie.

"Inglaterra, por favor," I said.

Miguel took another look at Marie and raised his eyebrows. The gringo is a fool.

I know it, I replied. Why had I made separate reservations for us? Idiot!

"It was worth waiting the extra time," she said, as the car swung left on to the highway into the city.

"Why?"

"I got on the phone. My Spanish isn't bad, I find."

"It's better when they can see you."

"That's what I mean. I did all of his over the phone."

"What?"

"You will see. I learned that the Hotel Colon is where a lot of the bullfighters stay. We'll want to hang out there a little."

"Particularly since your Spanish is so good."

"I won't need a ticket, by the way."

That evening, as I sat in my seat at the bullring, I looked down at the callejon—the area between the tendidos—the seats where the spectators sit—and the fence (or barrera) where the bulls are. I had great seats in fila one—first row, near a couple of old matadors, Paco Camino and Santiago Martin, "El Viti"—but Marie had done better. She held up the piece of plastic on a cord around her neck. It was a photographer's pass. I saw. Her Spanish was better than mine.

The Maestranza de Caballos in Sevilla may not be the oldest extant bullring in the world—Ronda's great stone plaza claims to have been built a few years earlier in the late 18th century—but its sand is the color of old gold and comes from a hillside south of the city. If it were not for a few aerials visible above the western edge of the ring, we would be back watching Belmonte, Gaona, and Joselito in 1915, or Manolete, Dominguin, and Pepe Luis Vasquez in 1945. The bells of the Giralda melted around the ring as if fitting themselves to its slightly egg-shaped circle and the clouds pillared above. I did not believe El Greco's clouds until I saw the Spanish sky over the Maestranza. Sevilla alone observes a decorum of silence. In Madrid, one section of spectators derides each matador loudly, and the others are usually chilly to all but the most splendid combination of art and heroism. In Pamplona, everyone seems to be drunk, so that man and bull alone are sober and about their rhythm of killing. In Sevilla, the quick drilling noise of a cellphone is an intrusion. If people are noisy, the hiss of "shuss, shuss" rises around like an audible fog. "Ole!" of course, coming unbidden, like the grunt when someone belts you in the stomach, is part of the rhythm, and it crescendos to a steady roar that can translate into a communal shriek when the matador is tossed or into an instant diminuendo if he misses with the sword. A miss after a good final section of the fight (faena) will draw a "Lastima!" from many. It means "Pity!" The other sound is that of the trumpets signaling the change from picadors to banderilleros to the final act of the matador. During a good faena, the band plays a pasodoble. For Finito de Cordoba, a brave young matador from up the river who is doing wonderful things with a brave bull, they play "Manolete." It is a supreme tribute, because Manolete is the greatest bullfighter ever to come from Cordoba. I wonder whether the young man, born some thirty years after Manolete was killed by a bull in Linares, recognizes the tune. In his concentration, he probably doesn't even hear it. When I played football, I could hear the occasional verb of the bass drum, but that was all. It was the clatter of equipment, "38 left on three," and the sound of your own breathing that you heard in that zone bounded by the sidelines.

For the rest of us, the silence of the ring insists on the evaluation of any sound. One can usually decode the sounds inside a stadium if he knows what game is being played, like Brutus and Cassius listening to Caesar play humility with his hands against the ambition surging in his heart. A homerun, a touchdown, a long pass that spirals incomplete into a sudden gasp of silence— the chorus tells you what the ball has done, but it is unusual to be within a crowd that listens like this, as opposed to just reacting to what it thinks it has seen. No sporting event invites the crowd into the rhythm of what is happening. It is not "We Want A Hit!" or the chant of cheerleaders. The "Oles" come an instant before the pass is completed. It is a rising reaction. The first pass of a series may be the best technically, but it merely begins a sequence that builds emotion in the eye, as music does in the ear, each sense a conduit to the passions. The first pass seldom draws more than a grunt of appreciation. The last—as the matador does a flamenco turn from the horns—should leave him the carpet of an ovation on which to prance away for the moment, while the bull catches the last of the several breaths remaining to it.

A handsome young man from Portugal, Pedrito, smiled as he took the small cape (muleta) to face his bull. He reminded me of one of Lorca's poems, about the dancer, Juan Breva. "Era la misma/ pera cantando/detras una sonrisa." "He was pain itself while/ he sang behind his smile." Pedrito knew the bull could kill him but Pedrito took chances as he worked with this one, cutting the distances between the horn and the man's legs and stomach to millimeters even as the bull begins to learn that it is not movement at which he should thrust but the still and shining shape beside the swing of that exasperating emptiness. The moment of the bull's complete education is also the moment of his death. Pedrito moved over the right horn and placed the sword perfectly. The bull's head came up and went through Pedrito's right leg—or so it seemed from where I sat, in the first row about twenty feet away. The woman next to me grabbed my hand.

The bull was dead, but the horn had torn a gigantic gash in Pedrito's suit of lights. He limped, but his femoral artery had not been severed, as Manolete's had been in Linares.

"He's okay," I said to the woman.

"Yes. Thank heavens!" she said in English.

She was not tracking me. It turned out that she owns a ganaderia in Mexico—a ranch that raises bulls. I tossed out the names of Mexican matadors—the graceful Alfredo Leal, the brave Jamie Rangel, the great Manolo Martinez, who also raised fighting bulls before he died a few years ago—all of this to confirm my credentials as aficionado.

The woman had the rich, pouty lips and brown eyes of Mexico. She wore an elegant tan suit of wool with lapels that swelled out from from her bosom.

"And, of course, my favorite was Luis Procuna," I said

I had watched an old black and white film called "Torero," about Procuna, so I could fake it knowledgeably about him.

A warmth suffused her eyes, as if I have named a former lover, momentarily forgotten in the excitement of a present moment. I had to remind myself that Marie was down there in the callejon taking pictures.

"Ah yes, the matador of sun and shadow. When he was good . . ."

And when he was bad—bolting from the bull and leaping the fence—he would wait until the next Sunday at El Toreo or the Plaza Mexico and all would be forgiven on a rising tide of oles.

Both Spanish and Mexican men and women—sometimes more the women, because they don't have to pretend a courage that is not even skin deep—live out a vicarious life through the matadors. Death—black, snorting, stinking of the corral, seeking resistance to one of its horns and ready to throw the other in an instant, like a spear—and the frail man, gleaming in green and gold, stand in for whatever smaller drama the people are playing out. They will die, but the man, touring the ring (clockwise in Spain) takes that time from them for a moment. It occurs in smaller moments—or non moments—when the cape seems to stop the bull for an instant, as if a frame of film has paused as it passes through the light. One sees it and does not believe that it has happened—that instant of stillness, of insight, of awareness that, yes, the corrida, in less than a second, makes time into something that is not to be feared. The instant goes, death turns again for another pass.

"See?" I asked the woman next to me, Mercedes of the Rio Dulce Ranch, below Guadalajara, as a beautiful lad named Abellan did a Gaonera, and froze the moment before the bull lashed past his ankles, horns picking up the light before driving into the shadow that now bisected the ring .

"Did you?"

"Yes."

"I sometimes don't think anyone else sees."

I had stood and cried out before I had taken in what I had seen. Instant replay is in the retinas. Response occurs before recognition. It is not like watching a homerun climb and lose itself in a fiery summer sky or in the few stars that show above the lights before dropping into a hungry nesting of woven hands. That is process. You measure the wind as the ball rises. It is not like watching a one-punch knockout—Louis-Braddock, Robinson-Fullmer, the first Marciano-Walcott, Weaver-Tate, Foreman-Moorer. That moment resembles a good kill in the bullring. Setting a man up for the left hook or right cross is a process, as is the kill in the corrida. It involves lowering the bull's head, as the hateful picadores drive a steel spear into the bull's shoulder muscles. It demands the positioning of the bull's forefeet close together so that the area between the shoulders is open for the sword. A matador will flick his muleta slightly and the bull will move a front foot a couple of inches in response. The matador must drive his sword (espada) between the shoulderblades so that the bull's aorta is destroyed. The dead bull has his last, best chance to get the matador at that moment by driving his right horn up into the man's femoral artery. The bullfighter can destroy his triumph by hitting bone with his sword.

I looked at the sky for a moment to tell myself that I had seen the mystery. It was a quite—where a bullfighter pulls the bull away from the horse after the pic, often with fancy capework. Abellan did a series of Gaoneras, where the matador holds the cape behind his hip. It can be a dangerous pass, because the suit of lights gleams in front of the bull and only the movement of the cape pulls the bull past the exposed body of the man. As the bull went past everything stopped for a moment—the swing of the cape and the drive of the bull's horn past the man's pink stockings. It was scarcely palpable, but it was there—a stopping of time itself.

"He's starting off with naturales," I said to the woman.

Naturales are passes made with the left hand, so that the bull's left horn is the one that goes by the matador. They are more dangerous than right handed passes, because they hold less of the muleta out to the bull, but, with the veronica, they are the basic passes of the bullring, the ones whereby matadors are judged regardless of what other fancy work they may do.

"Yes. He can see that the bull prefers the right horn."

"How can he see that?"

I had wondered what it was that matadors stared at so intently as they watched the bull come out of the corral and make its initial moves around the ring.

"This bull begins its charge with its right leg. That tells which horn he favors."

I saw her glance at my face.

My nose had been broken some years ago by a very good left jab from a very good light heavyweight during a one-sided fight in the intercollegiate semi-finals. While the nose was not smashed into my face, it had been shifted to the side and a nob of cartilage glowed white at the point of rearrangement. It set me apart at white tie affairs, saying, here is a man who has been places we have not. It made me one with working men, saying, here is a man who has been were we have—that is, if I did not show my left hand, which had merely tossed a tennis ball into the air for years. The nose did seem to be an attractor of attractive women. I used it as a version of situational ethics, fitting my persona around it depending on where I was and who I perceived was looking at it. I don't know whether other people create such shifting perspectives of themselves. I've never dared ask. I do know that most other people, though they may be fabricating identities as they go, don't give much of a damn about other people.

I had known it was time to quit when I woke up taking a shower and asked, "What round did he knock me out?"

The guy next to me, a welterweight from Springfield with hair all over his body said, "Are you shittin' me? It was close. You even landed a good left hook in the third."

Twenty five years ago. That third round would never be available to memory.

I came back. I saw Marie talking to an old man in the callejon. That was Cano, the famous bullfight photographer. He was 84 and still took pictures that showed precisely the relationship between horn, cape, and man.

He was pointing, and Marie was nodding, as if she understood what he was saying, photographer to photographer.

He looked at her camera. It was a Nicon. It did everything—focused, zoomed in and out, made rack shots, adjusted for light.

He smiled and nodded. I wondered what he had begun with. An old Kodak, probably. His pictures of Manolete, Ortega, Arruza, and the veronica of Gitanillo de Triana, though, had stopped motion even as they showed motion what it was. You sensed in his photographs the next moment in the frame, even though that moment would never come.

Everyone would have his own metaphor if he could see past the blood pulsing down the black hide of the animal. Mine is easy. I am being followed. I may be in danger. I didn't know a damned thing. But did they—the very specific they, whoever they were—know that I knew nothing? Somehow, whatever danger I am in is insignificant, as long as the men out there in that golden space, now circumscribed by shadow, are standing in for me. Of course, I wish I hadn't brought Marie along on this trip. I'd do better by myself. I laugh. It is not because this beautiful Mexican woman is next to me. It is because I have put Marie in danger. I did find myself wondering just a bit what Mercedes made of my smashed up nose.

Marie looked up at me and smiled. We were not supposed to acknowledge each other—for safety's sake. I saw her glance at the woman to my right. Marie nodded. Glad you are having *some* fun out of this! I would catch up with Marie later at the Inglaterra.

The way to Malaga in the early morning was a filling up with light. I had never seen it come this way, over the rows of sunflowers, over the olive trees that marched up the mountainsides and down again, into the fields, where a single tree would accept the flood around its knees and begin to cast a shadow again, along the windrows like water released from an unseen lake, and then the sweep down the highway toward Malaga, with the full day holding the sea up in golden hands. I was giving a lecture at the University, a grim pile of concrete set on top of a carved-out hillside along a highway that looked like California, where I first picked up my check and then went back into the city to cash it. In the strange ways of Spain—or perhaps it was only the Spanish academic community—the check had to be made out to me. Only I could cash it, and that feat could be accomplished only at the bank that served La Universidad de Malaga. My host, an amiable man I had met at one of my rare premiers, introduced me and told me he would be back in half an hour, in time to get me to my talk—"The Case for Verse Drama," which made much of the recent influx of Shakespeare films as a basis for my case. I thought about the talk and glanced at my notes—it is sometimes impossible to see notes when suddenly you are at a lectern with a light in your face and a damned microphone craning down—as I sat in a small room awaiting the momentous cashing of my check. Well, hell, it was enough for four nights at the Alfonso at $450 a night , and it was mine to spend.

The trip to Malaga was part of my cover. Two of my plays had been translated into Spanish with some success. Hardly Lope de Vega or Calderon, but they were "academic" plays based on classical themes, and had actually been studied in the classrooms. I was, therefore, more interested in this lecture than in the assignment—except for what the assignment paid. I could still hear Roger Baldwin's bullying voice on the phone, much more real than any sense that he would speak no more. I did not realize how treacherous he was—had been—in sending me to Spain, but that day in Malaga made it true. It was as if Baldwin had set it up. Had it not been for Malaga, I am certain that Marie and I would have returned to Los Estados Unidos without incident. I knew that someone had been watching me. After Malaga, they had a reason to watch.

I have always had the bad habit of overhearing things I am not supposed to hear. Once a conversation begins, though, one cannot cough to announce one's presence. And—sometimes—what is being said is interesting.

Voices in rapid and occasionally angry Spanish came through the thin partition to my right. I could see two shadows through the frosted glass.

"I do not want that much money coming through this bank, Jorge. We are a small bank. People will have questions."

"Why, Manuel? It is solid Banco Hemisphero money. It hasn't come from Cyprus."

Cyprus? Oh, yes, that's where the Colombian drug lords laundered their money.

"I know that. And then another sum—not quite so huge, perhaps three quarters, perhaps half, comes back."

"And goes quickly."

"Do you think people cannot draw conclusions? Records do exist. It is not a matter of the speed of transaction."

"But they connect nothing with nothing, Manuel. We have been chosen for this sequence of transactions precisely because we are small."

"Let them choose a bank in Portugal."

"Don't you think they will? Why do you think Portugal is holding out against accepting the European banking regulations? They want this business. It is worth . . ."

"I know what it's worth, Jorge. They believe that's all we think of. Profit, greed."

"We are in business."

"And we are doing well by honest means."

"Nothing dishonest . . ."

"You mean it is within the law as it exists, as you interpret that law? That is not . . ."

They both paused. I looked away as a shadow moved toward me, growing darker in the frosted glass.

The door to the next room opened.

"Ah, senor." It was the oily Jorge. "You have been waiting?"

I pretended not to understand him. I mimed the writing of a check.

"A check?"

"Si, si," I said.

"Un momento."

He said something into the next room.

"Senor Telefilo, un momento, por favor."

Jorge came with me, returned me my passport after examining it with some care—to make sure he knew my name—and counted my money into my palm in exaggerated English.

I left, my purse full of pesetas, and feeling that I had a large red bullseye in the center of my back. As I waited at the entrance for my host, I noticed the flowershops in the park between the two sections of the boulevard. I thought—they are not selling flowers for birthdays or weddings. They are selling flowers for funerals.

My host, Jose Ramon, had told me that I should visit the "Luces de Sangre" exhibit at the Museo Municipal before I left, so I had my driver swing down the Paseo de Reding, across the Rio Guadalmedina, past La Malaguenta, the Plaza de Toros, and under the crenellated shadows of the Catillo de Gibrafaro, built by Badis, Ziri of Granada in the 11th century, on the mountainside that overlooked the port in which the white-walled cruise ships slumbered against the hazy mirage of the Mediterranean beyond. I had plenty of time to get back to Sevilla, and my pose as aficionado demanded a brief side trip, in this case a pilgrimage to look at the works of art that the bullring had produced: Goya, Manet, Picasso, and the lesser "blood lights."

I looked at a painting of a corrida in Ronda by Jose Solana. The clock tower below the waiting bells of the city hall said it was almost seven thirty, time for the bull to die in harmony with the red tile roofs and the red borders of the Spanish flags painted on the walls around the ring and flying above the heads of the mules waiting to drag the bull from the ring and the red of the muleta the matador held in front of the bull's glazing eyes. But the point of the painting, indicated by the line of afternoon shadow riding down a whitewashed wall was the matador's right hand, held up, palm out. It was covered with blood, meaning that he had put the sword in up to the bull's shoulderblades. And there it was, red hilt just visible above the droop of the banderillas. Spain—a brown hillside—shrugged above the scene.

 I felt time quiver for a moment from that hand—was it supposed to be Belmonte's, Ortega's, Nino de la Palma's? I recognized it. It was the face of the great killer of bulls, Diego Mazquiaran, "Fortuna," who killed a bull that had escaped the pens in Madrid in 1928 and died mad only twelve years later. I could feel the sun come down into the city and touch a distant window. I sensed a cave painting there in the dimness of the second floor of the museum, the horns pale against the rock. I was a visitor, awaiting an audience at the Palace of Knossos, suddenly understanding a lost language. And, yet, as centuries melted, I also felt that I was being watched, as if the prehistory had eyes of its own. It was more than just the general awareness of scrutinizing eyes that I had sensed since Montreal.

 I came back into the 20th century as I looked at the next canvas, Diaz's "Toreros saludando." One matador, hat off, head bowed to the Juez—the judge of the bullring, who holds the matador's chances for success in his hands—as if praying. And so he is, of course. The ceremonies of a given Sunday afternoon, from Madrid to some dusty square in a mountain village, manifest a religion free of guilt and the need for mercy, but inevitably filled with the agony that the Spanish give that dying man on the wood. In the ring, a shape armed with horns moved past a man who gleamed in the sun and held a frail cloth in front of those horns. The man might die, he might not. If he did not, he might have achieved a momentary victory over death, over the annihilation the Spaniards believed in in the streets outside the cathedrals.

 If he did poorly, even if he survived, he heard the whistles that shrieked of his shame. He had only lived to remind the spectators of the shambling reality of what usually happens to them during the days before they die. Except on the very rare occasion when the judge granted an indulto, the bull always died.

The next painting looked like a sculpture made of scraps of tin. It was a man on horseback. The horse was girded with a peto and had a long neck and outstretched head, as if trying to escape from its body. The man held a long stick in his right hand.

"Picador"—it captured the ridiculousness and the metallic menace of this reviled but necessary figure of the bullring.

I felt a shoulder beside my own.

"Senor Kane, you have many friends."

"I'm delighted to know that."

"We can do nothing at this point."

"I assumed as much."

"Luck."

"La Mancha is north of here, I understand," I said, gesturing toward Jose Cabellero's "Picador."

The next painting, by Aranda, showed the Maestranza in Sevilla, in the late 19th century, before its upper tier had been completed. Elegant men looked down from a private box. A girl in a white gown looked down at a fan she had dropped. It was Rembrandt—a bright figure, oblivious to the occasion, dominates whatever it is the men are doing.

The man had drifted toward a collage of bullfight items—old posters, a sword, banderillas, and a photograph of Joselito, smiling and holding the horn of a bull gingerly in his hand. Oh yes, one of the posters was from Talavera de la Reina, 16 de Mayo, 1920, Toros, Viuda de Ortega. One of those little bulls would kill him that day.

As I left the museum, I thought about those words. You have many friends. Was that a threat?—your friends would be saddened by your premature demise? It would fit the Spanish technique of indirection, and it would incorporate the grim Spanish version of irony, like the chief of the Civil Guards whom Pablo orders to kneel before he is shot. The policeman says that, yes, it is closer to the ground, but no one laughs.

No—it had been a wish for luck. That was also typically Spanish. Its terrain engendered fatalism. Under the shadow of the man twisted on the cross paganism did better than survive.

But—why? I was going to take Marie and get the hell out of Spain as soon as I did a few more things. I was not going to tilt at windmills and get knocked from my knock-kneed horse.

At noon the next day, the first edge of tropical heat had simmered across from Morocco with the warmth that such a first day always brings. I had slipped some coins into my pocket to search out a news stand which would have the *International Herald Tribune*. Someone had filched the hotel's copy before I had a chance to steal it myself. Like rocks under the spirit of streams, the streets simmered in the summer sun. All perspectives melted and bled down the cobbles like houses in dreams, burning with slow invisible fire. "Hace calor!" the natives said. Even they called it warm this day, sliding shadows of desire into corners waiting for the night. Senor! Senor! the beggar cried. I had mistaken a pound for a hundred pesetas, out of sight in my cosmopolitan pocket, no joke to him, as heat folded into his teeth, his Fortuna riding an inward breath. The poor are always food for smoke. I decided that the cool tiles of the Alfonso Trece were preferable to the steamy alley ways of the Barrio Santa Cruz. But I was close to "El Gallo" and I sat in the murmur of the courtyard and had a few beers. Whatever happened in the world yesterday would wait until tomorrow for me to find it out.

Marie and I sat in the living room portion of her suite at the Inglaterra—407-409—eating smoked salmon sandwiches and drinking Surena beer.

"Look, Larry, this is a great assignment, wonderful fun to be in Spain, smell the bulls, and all of that . . ."

"You don't have the cigar smoke."

"You think they aren't smoking those foul torpedoes down in the callejon? The stuff gathers like fog in a low lying field. It's like the goddamned Western Front in 1917. It's in my best blouses! But you are, as always, trying to divert me."

"No," I said, filling my mouth with smoked salmon.

"What I mean is, it's the kind of fast-paced working arrangement that doesn't leave any real space for us."

"Of course it does."

"You mean that in half an hour, we'll take our clothes off, lay them carefully on that sofa next to the bed, and climb between those clean sheets, to scuff them, dampen them, say crazy words to them . . ."

"Well, aren't we?"

"Of course. I mean time in which we tell each other who were are, who we want to be with each other—not just what the hell we are doing."

"We will."

"It's what a man always promises, isn't it. But the future never comes."

"Right now, my dear one, I think we are in danger."

"So you say. When you say 'my dear one' I know I'm in trouble. Existentially, we are always in danger, aren't we?"

"Yeah, but I mean immediate danger."

"We still have some things to do here."

"Exactly."

"All right, then . . ."

"In a couple of days, we'll go where you want to go."

"You decide."

"Okay. I'll get two tickets—to somewhere, and we'll go there."

She looked at me skeptically over the rim of her glass of beer.

Another emotional crisis averted, I thought. I was also quietly elated, of course—I had the emotional dynamics suddenly under my control. It was she who was asking for commitment. The dominant male needs to dominate. What I did not know was that our unknown destination was itself a lot further in the future than I knew then. Well, that is the nature of unknown destinations. It was my *chosen* destination that lay further off. And it was turned out not to be what I would have chosen at that moment. It turned out not to be Rome, Paris, London.

I noticed that the light, which had glittered before on the trajes de luces—the suits of light—of the matadors, was now weaving inside the golden threads as if the men had internalized the moment somehow. I looked up. Darkness had packed itself around the bowl of the plaza, and the lights were on. I had not noticed. I must be careful. Concentration on one thing, on one place, could be dangerous. An L1011 had crashed in the Everglades because the cockpit crew became fixated on a warning light that was malfunctioning. Cuidado! I had to keep saying that to myself as I watched the matadors pull the horns past their legs and bellies.

The matador from Portugal, Pedrito, jumped up and down on his toes after he had put he sword deep between the bull's shoulders. He drove the tension down into the sand—burying one more time what a moment before threatened to bury him. Death was not even slow-motion. It was arrested. The blade paused above the whirlpool of blood coming up to meet it. Movement continued. Like a photographer, I remembered the stillness. Had anyone else seen it? Or—not seen it, since it was an instant of stasis, of nonaction? Motion continued then, and I felt pursued again.

I looked down. Marie was in the callejon.

We had agreed not to communicate with each other, but she looked up, saw me looking at her, and pointed to her camera.

She had not only seen the moment, she had gotten it on film, captured that frozen instant forever.

Mercedes and I were seated together again the next afternoon. Obviously, this block of very good tickets had been sold to the consierjes of the better hotels for further sale to their wealthy guests. It was an afternoon on which rain clouds made moorish castles in the green Guadalquivir. I was asking her about her ranch and the bulls.

A bull charged into the ring and turned to the left. The crowd cheered.

"That looks like a good one," Mercedes said.

"Why?"

"It's not a trotter. A bull that trots around is seldom any good. This one favors the left horn, so Pedrito will have to work hard to give it a good series of naturales, but that's his way to an ear. He can get one with this bull."

But then the bull charged the entrance to the callejon and ripped its left horn off. Blood came from the horn, and the bull leaped about in agony.

Mercedes had grabbed my hand.

"They say that in Mexico, the matador is more important and that in Spain, it's the bulls. It is not so."

The steers came out, their bells clattering, and attempted to get the bull back out of the gate.

"Poor animal!" I said.

"Yes. Even if it would have been dead in another fifteen minutes. I have heard that there are animal rights people here in Sevilla doing research. That would be a bull on their side, as they see things."

"Even if it was an accident?"

"It would not have happened had the animal not been removed from its natural habitat."

"But cattle are raised to be slaughtered."

"That makes no difference to those people."

"Yes, there's no logic to it."

The damaged bull, bellowing in pain, finally disappeared up the dark passage from which he had come moments before.

"You are interested in the animals," she said.

I was one of those investigators. I was an impostor, someone who had sneaked into the ceremony to discredit it. I was worse than a heretic. I was a despoiler of the consecrated wine of the Mass.

"I understand the position," she said. "But it is misplaced when it comes to the bulls."

"I agree."

Her head pivoted slowly toward me.

"You have learned that much?"

I had, after all, been posing as someone who loved the bullfights. I had watched film and read a few books in the few days between the assignment in Montreal and the supposed pilgrimage to the shrine of Maestranza, but now I had seen them.

"You are in a difficult position, then," she said. I was—but how did she know?

"Not really. I merely file my report. I can be neutral, dispassionate."

The next bull came out, trotted around, and sought to go back into the cool darkness of the corrals.

"Double pity now," Mercedes said.

"I move in certain circles," she said, staring at the dull gold of sand under cloud, as if studying the proclivities of this bull.

"You should be careful. If you are working for that man who is staying at the Colon, you should be very careful. Come visit my ranch in Mexico."

"I will."

The trotter was in the process of refusing to charge the horse. People whistled. The judge considered whether to call in the steers again. The corrida can be a perverse place. This is the toro that should have damaged its horn, but this one would not have attacked the fence.

Rain came suddenly, with a moan from the side across the ring from us. Up went black umbrellas, so that the other side looked like mourners making a parachute drop to a funeral. The rain spattered across the sand.

"We can share this," Mercedes said, opening her umbrella with a hollow thump and holding it up.

I looked along the callejon. Marie was getting a photograph of a banderillero, face bleak in waterdrops, staring at his matador's bull.

The rain meant nothing. The horns—even of a cowardly bull—could still kill, even if not gleaming in the late afternoon sun, even if gray with rain.

The elevator door swung open, framing three men about to step into the circular marble lobby of the Hotel Colon. Marie got the picture. A man who had been in the elevator, behind the three principals, come over to her.

"Give me the film, please," he said quietly, in Spanish.

She fumbled with her camera for a moment and handed him a roll of film.

"Thank you," the man said, bowing, slipping the roll of film into his suit jacket, and turning toward the steps down to the street.

The others had gone in separate directions immediately. A Frenchman in a green silk blazer and silk scarf went to the restaurant on one side of the lobby. The Spaniard in the cream colored suit walked through the smoky lobby to the bar on the other side, and the American in a pinstriped suit strode out to the street, where a limo purred. It was as if they had come down together in the elevator by coincidence. The photograph, however, would have proved to anyone that they were coming down from a business meeting in one of the salons on the mezzanine.

I could have been wrong about the nationality of the Frenchman. He could have been Belgian. But the Picasso-bulge of the Spaniard's eyes was obvious, and one gringo can tell when another gringo is in the room. The American's eyes had swung through the drift of smoke toward me as he had started down the marble steps. I thought I had seen him somewhere, or perhaps it was just his swagger—Mike Todd. Gotti, Milken, Hollywood, Mafia, Wall Street. He was an American of the type who should at least have the grace to stay home, but lacks grace altogether.

The man who had taken Marie's roll of film followed the American out to the limo.

"Too bad about the film," I said, as we turned into the Plaza Nuevo.

"Just film."
"I wonder who those guys were?"
"Who they are, you mean. I hope we don't find out."

The Casa Robles tells its customers that they can enjoy "sabor andaluz en su mesa"—Andalusian flavor on your table. Marie had talked me into the turbot filled with prawn and spinach. Even the brussel sprouts were good.

"What's in this sauce?"

Marie licked her lips and rolled her dark eyes back as if consulting a list of ingredients.

"Nothing unusual. Onion, garlic, white wine, broth from the fish. It is, as usual, the balancing that makes the difference."

The restaurant was filled with works of art, an eclectic collection—vast canvases depicting saints about some miracle or other, Andalusian primitives, austere El Greco faces straining against the tug of their souls, and an occasional statue. Our quiet table sat beneath the marble bust of a Greek warrior, his helmet pulled back onto the luxurious curls of his head.

"How did that speech go again?"
"Which one?"
"Where he talks about dreaming and waking up."

> "Oh yeah—
> 'I dream of taking back that word again,
> Of turning to ten thousand men in bronze
> to say that nothing is worth this sacrifice.
> But I did not. And then I wake again.
> No oblivion waits for us down in
> the world of shades, for it is like the drift
> of fog in which we cannot see but feel
> the error of a lifetime sharper than
> the knives that did me in when I returned
> and strode the carpet . . .'"

"It's you."

"Agamemnon to Iphigenia. It does have a subtext."

"As long as you are aware."

"We writers are aware. People who don't think so wish they were what they call 'creative.' That's why they hope that what writers do is unconscious."

"Instead of just damned hard work."

"It is that, Marie. But not just that. If it were just that . . ."

"I know. I do know that. I notice you finished your turbot."

"Why so I did! Now that was an unconscious activity!"

"I think that's Achilles."

"I think it is. Unconscious all the way. He did not live into the age of regret."

I left Marie at the Inglaterra and walked across the Plaza. San Fernando held a cross forward to pigeons and shoppers. The people did not pause to ask what that was in the statue's hand. For the pigeons it was a convenient landing place. Below the Saint, one pigeon stood on the gauntlet of a knight, pretending to be a falcon. Even birds pretend. I was pretending to be an animal rights researcher while pretending to be an aficionado. I thought about the three men in the elevator. It was warm in the center of the Plaza, yet I shivered. The heads under the pedestal on which the statue stood looked like skulls, etched and bleached under centuries of Sevillian heat and rain. The cross extended out into years that showered and shone upon it but were as aware of it as the people and the pigeons in the Plaza.

It is not easy to get in to a *sorteo*. That is the process whereby the managers of the matadors pick out the bulls that will be fought later in the afternoon. Since each matador fights two bulls, the managers try to pair the bulls as best they can—a smaller one with short horns with a larger one with more dangerous armament. To be there is to be an insider, which I definitely was not. About fifteen thousand pesetas later, however, I had a small piece of purple cardboard with a "Maestranza" stamp on it.

"Hola! Buenas dias!"

The man in the sun-folded face sitting on a canvas stool glanced at the card and flicked a grainy thumb over his shoulder.

I did not know where to go, but strode confidently to the left of the entrance, where I knew the corrals were located. I heard voices and went up some wooden steps. Men were standing around a platform, elbows on a rail, looking down at a hoof-roughened space of empty dirt. The air was full of the smell of cigar and urine-soaked wood .

I nodded, trying to look like an eminent foreign journalist they had not heard about.

I could hear the trucks backing up to the gate outside the ring in the area just off the Paseo de Cristobal Colon. The hiss of brakes was followed by a snort and a hollow clomping as each bull emerged from the close darkness of the truck to the lengthy darkness of a tunnel. Gates on pulleys squealed open and shut. Heavy bolts snapped against their outer metal and clunked into their locks, and always came the sound of hooves, and snorting, and the scrape of horn against wood.

Finally, a black shape with a twin gleam of horns came into the empty space below us. He stared into the angle of light coming down from Asia Minor, dropped his head, twisted back in the direction he had come, and drove a horn into the now closed gate. The brief upward stroke scraped the green surface down to the wood, a space an inch wide and two feet long.

How, I wondered, could you kill such a creature? Not why. That was easy. This was a dangerous animal. Muy pelegroso. But how?

I looked at the list of the names of the bulls.

This one was Amigocito. Little friend. About 1350 pounds of friendship.

The men near me were jabbering.

"Yes," one said. "I'll take him if you let me pick the other one."

"How can I do that. We haven't seen the others?"

The other man shrugged. It was the Spanish shrug—not the

New York shoulders of sheer indifference, but the show of Iberian scorn.

"Under condition, then," the man said.

I looked again at the list of the bulls. Something had caught my eye. Yes, under the list of substitute bulls. "Bailador."

I touched the elbow of the man next to me and pointed at the name.

"The name of the bull that killed Joselito at Talavera."

I was surprised that any ranch would recycle the name of the little, nearsighted bull that had destroyed Spain's most secure bullfighter, in 1920. Miura, the man whose bull killed Manolete in 1947, had been so angry that he killed the bull's mother. The head of "Islera" hung above the exit of the bullfight museum in Sevilla, a few yards from where I stood. The head of the killer, "Islero," had not been saved, even though his hide was preserved behind a glass case in Cordoba, Manolete's hometown.

The man said nothing.

"Sanchez Mejias killed him," I said.

Joselito's brother-in-law, alternating with Joselito that day, had killed Bailador, after watching his wife's brother die in that desert place.

"Mama! Mama! I'm smothering!" Joselito had said.

This time the man glanced at me and nodded.

This is one of those gringos who knows about bullfighting. At least that's what I hoped he was saying. I felt very much out of place as these superb animals from Victoriano Martin came blackly out of darkness into this rectangle of sun and shadow and disappeared into the labyrinth again, waiting for that burst into the golden afternoon that would quickly turn to blood pulsing down the midnight hide. I was being watched, of course, and this time it was not paranoia. I was in a secret place within a secular sanctuary—the home of Spanish bullfighting, the place where Chincuelo had invented the Chinculina, most beautiful of cape passes, where the great ones have held their monteras up to the thousand faces of Sevilla and to the thousands of hands clapping like the beaks of so many hungry birds—Joselito, Belmonte, Gitanillo de Triana, Manolete, Paquirri, three of them killed in the ring—Talavera, Linares, Pocoblanco. Gitanillo was there in Linares when his great friend Manolete died. Gitanillo vowed never to fight a bull again, and he never did. Perhaps it was the smell of the place that made the research necessary for me to pretend to be an aficionado de los toros suddenly come alive as memory.

The *sorteo* was over. The man next to me touched my arm.

"You are writing about this?" he asked, in Spanish.

I must be quick. He has something to tell me. I cannot protest too much, either.

"No," I said. "I am just an interested Norteamericano."

"Venga conmigo."

I followed him down some steps on the other side of the corral.

"Mejias was my great-great uncle," he said, as if explaining why he had befriended me.

"No one likes this," he said, "but the matadors will not fight otherwise."

We were in a small room, misty in cigar smoke. A bull's head appeared at a wooden window. A small gate dropped, like the headpiece of the stocks, and two men pushed boards into the bull's neck to immobilize him. It was "Amigocito."

A man with a circular saw cut two inches from the bull's horn. Amigocito's eyes widened and he moaned as the saw screamed though. This was a painful process, perhaps like getting a fingernail torn off. As another man filed the horn back into a point, the room was filled with the keening heat of shavings. The bull moaned. This really is cruel, I thought. Torture.

A third man applied a sticky, pitchlike substance to the reformed horns and polished them with a cloth. The horns looked like new, but they had been weakened. Many bulls come into the ring with splintered horns, because they have tried their new configuration and found that has lost its tensile strength in the process of "afiecto." The reason why the head of "Islero," the bull that killed Manolete, was not retained is because it, too, had had its horns cut down and reshaped. Even that mutilated right horn was enough to kill Manolete.

The bull would come into the ring in pain, and further handicapped by its inability to know where the tip of its horn was. It would be as you reached for something with a suddenly shortened hand.

I had looked at the corrida's heart of darkness. I remembered that Pope Alexander VI—Rodrigo Borgia—on becoming Pope in 1492, had not celebrated a mass of consecration but had presided over a bullfight in which five bulls were killed. This was sacrilege so close to the mystery to be ritually enacted later in the day, when Little Friend would die within that slowing of time which conferred a momentary immortality upon my own transcience. I had become an aficionado, I realized, and could only object to this cruelty within the larger pattern of pain and inevitable death.

"Bastante," I said. "I have seen enough."

The man nodded. Why had he brought me here?—to initiate me into something that challenged my blue-eyed wonder? Perhaps. I looked at him again. I had seen him somewhere before.

He nodded and gestured toward the steps.

I left. It was a relief to get out of the dusty heat of that interior room. As I came out through the iron side gate of the Plaza, past the old man sitting on his canvas stool, and into the sun pulling shadows into the trees along the river, I realized where I had seen that man. He was one of the men in the picture Marie had taken, the photo confiscated by the big bodyguard. Yes, those bulging Picasso eyes were impossible to forget.

Did he know that I was posing as an aficionado, but was really doing a piece on cruelty to animals? I had confused myself. I was a Jew disguised in a Gestapo uniform, who had come to believe in what the Gestapo was doing. What the motives of others could be was even more confusing. My visit to that inner chamber had something to do with my overhearing a conversation in Malaga. And that could not be good.

When in doubt, walk purposefully, as if you know where you are going. That used to be the advice they gave people in strange cities. What a thief or mugger looks at are shoes, eyes, haircut, location of wallet or purse. The vigor of the stride has nothing to do with anything. I walked purposefully, however, past a few people coming out of the meeting room. I wanted to look as if I had forgotten something. A heavy-set man in a suit stood against the portal that led into the room.

"Hola," I said, conveying what I hoped was the right balance of democratic respect for a fellow human being and superiority of status.

The long table ran down from a magnificent mural of Columbus's ships—the Nina, the Pinta, and the Andrea Doria—under crystal chandeliers. No one was there. Amid the dishevelment of a meeting adjourned—the half-empty bottles of water, the drying rings of glasses in the green table covering, the scattered pencils—were pads of paper, rich creamcolored pads with "Alfonso XIII" on the top. I gathered them up and left the room.

A few had doodles that would have given me plenty to evaluate had I been a reader of circles, rhomboids, and floral designs, and a few had the indentations of writing. Some of the indentations were similar to those Olivia had shown me. "Protest." "Missile Defense." Others were new, but equally puzzling. "Aids Research X." "Jap Monetary Policy +." The latter notation, at least, had something to do with the ostensible purpose of this meeting of the Western European section of the Planetary Organization. "Poppy Spray. Enc." "London" with a hyphen linking the name of the city to a picture of a hot dog. If I could get that document . . .

We sat in The Trinity Pub of the Hotel Inglaterra. The hotel had a black London cab outside the door, and a huge stuffed Redcoat in a beaver sitting in an outsized chair in the lobby. Just inside the blue-tiled margins of the lobby, the pub had paneled walls, dark benches and tables, barstools cushioned in blue and red patterns, photos of Dublin, and Samuel Beckett's Trinity College cape—

where had they stolen that?—to give Paddy a taste of the old sod here in this intensely Spanish city.

I was having a half lager, half stout, while Marie sipped at a Trinity 00, some combination of run and liquor that I did not deign to sample.

I went out to the men's room.

Another slid up beside me at the adjoining urinal. I don't like that—inevitable as it is—perhaps because it awakens my latent homophobia. Yes, live and let live, don't discriminate, but don't tell me what I have to like and dislike personally.

Just as I reached for the valve above the porcelain, the man said to me, "Your woman is very pretty."

Su mujer es muy bonita.

I left without a word.

That had been a threat. It had to be. I half expected Marie to be gone as I turned the corner, but she was there, lips on her straw, eyes raised in my direction. Muy bonita!

I did not want anything to happen to her.

"Happy St. Patrick's Day," she said.

"Yeah." I said. "That's in March isn't it?"

"Another beer?"

"You want another of those concoctions?"

"No. Not New Year's Eve quite yet, either."

"No. That's it for me."

Let the Irish vessel lie, empty of its poetry.

I said the line out loud.

"I like that."

"Trochee by Auden," I said. "Let's . . ."

"Yes, let's," she said.

I am not one of those North Americans who sees himself as a matador. The vicarious does not translate for me into fantasy. I doubt that there's ever been a blue-eyed bullfighter. There was a Chinese bullfighter—Vincente Hong—who is the only matador I know of who actually cut a pigtail to begin his career. In the old days, matadors actually grew a pigtail (a coleta) that they cut when they retired. The last one I know of to do that was the great Mexican, Luis Procuna, in 1974. I admit that occasionally I sketch a derachazo in the air with my right hand or translate the taking off of my raincoat into a media veronica—but there is no toro there, no snort as he drives into illusion, no sifting of sand under his hooves, no smell of bull or of his blood or of my own sweat juicing the expensive suit with fear. I could not do it, therefore admire the men who can, and hate the fear of those who go out there and cannot.

And sometimes you see both, almost simultaneously. Juan Padilla, a stocky little matador from Jerez, kneels in front of the gate from which the bull will emerge. He will perform a larga cambiada, where he swings the cape over his head as the bull charges. If he does it too soon, the bull reverses and nails him. If he does it too late, the bull has no chance to swerve.

"He's too close," I say.

"Much too close," Mercedes says. "He should be at least as far out as that first circle in the sand."

The bull comes out of the dark corridor into the sunlight. He picks Padilla up and cartwheels him for fifty feet across the ring before the others can distract the animal. Padilla's suit of lights has been slashed, and his left leg is gashed. He is carried to the infirmeria. Mercedes lets go of my hand. We will not see Padilla again this afternoon.

But we do. A buzz and then cheering greets him as his dark head comes back along the passage way.

And then he dies again—or so it seems. He goes in to kill the bull and is thrown into the air. He gets up, covered with blood, and staggers into the arms of one of his banderilleros. I think—he has been gored in the chest and is about to die. I am a few feet from him and I look at his eyes, to catch what he sees just before the opaque moment of death. But it is only his wind that has been knocked out, and it is the bull's blood that covers his shirt. He gets an ear.

The other matadors—Tato and J. A. Campuzano—are afraid of the bulls. These are Miuras, and, as Miuras always do, they look as if they have been fought before. They look from cape to man, man to cape, as if making a selection. I don't blame the matadors for being afraid, but they are getting paid a 20% premium for fighting the Miuras—an extra $60 000 for the afternoon. Tato and Campuzano are intent on showing that the animals cannot be fought. That is a self-fulfilling prophecy that Padilla has already refuted. Tato and Campuzano make a few punishing passes, twisting the bulls around on their own axis, then dispatch the animals safely by stabbing them in the lungs. The crowd jeers and throws cushions at the two discredited matadors. Padilla is in the infirmary being treated for broken ribs.

Someone shouts "Cobarde!"—coward—and Tato spins. The man puts his right hand on his testicles and repeats the word. Tato turns away. His check will still be good.

But even during bad bullfights, I relax and enjoy the couple of hours. Nothing will happen to me here. Danger may rush back and forth out there on those metallic sands, but I am safe here in the barrera. I can hear the birds, sounding as if they are stringing beads above the ring, and the bells of the city, a final fragment of a bronze circle, the phantom touch of an antique coin, touching the northern edge of the Plaza and its tiles, on fire with sunset. The sounds are older than the bullring, and they seem to have shaped the place to their design, as if the bells had built a physical echo of their circularity.

When I am alone, I tend to think of my failed marriage—that failure was built-in, but who sees that soon enough?—and of my daughter, Katherine. All I had to do was to take care of her. That one small mission in life, and I had failed it. At what point do you start pulling a load of regret with you as the drift toward the waterfall gets stronger? I have this metaphor of the river. It goes back to Heraclitus. At some point that giant waterfall begins to assert its pull and the current wrinkles into a series of grins and the laughter begins to echo back along the banks on either side, and there is not a damned thing you can do about it. At times, I cannot interrupt myself with this or that to keep that kind of thinking at bay. I say thinking. It is a vague combination of memory and intuition. You can't think when you are alone. You need stimulus. Camus is right—the alternative to any other decision is suicide.

So, I was happy when the phone rang.

The steps down to the lobby had begun to hollow after seventy years and I noticed my hand on the wooden railing. I was not as sure of my step as I was—yesterday.

I recognized him, of course, facing me from one of the tables that run in a line inside the glass partition that divides the hotel from its central courtyard. He was dressed in one of those subtle gray suits that Spaniards wear so well.

"Of course, I remember you, Senor."

"Do you care for coffee?"

"A Cruzcampo would be fine."

"You like Spanish beer?"

"I come from a huge country, Senor Telefilo, that can make a good beer only in small quantities. Anchor Steam of the West Coast and a host of micro-breweries elsewhere. The rest? I will not offend you by describing it. The problem, of course, is that Americans drink it so quickly and copiously that they don't taste it as it goes down. Yes, you know how to make a good beer. So do the Mexicans."

"You understand Spain quite well."

He sipped at his coffee, his austere face veiled in steam for a moment.

"What is it you think I understand?"

"We are still suffering from the memories of violence. In Palma Del Rio . . ."

"Where El Cordobes lived."

"Yes, and I too. My grandfather and all his family were killed. Almost all. My grandmother managed to hide my father with a peasant family. He lived with them for three years, until 1939."

"I have read about what happened."

I had read *For Whom the Bell Tolls*, finally a sentimental work but vivid in its description of the executions of the landed gentry of Ronda.

"There was violence after 1939."

"Yes."

Franco's retribution—I had read Sartre's "The Wall," as well.

"We did not go into World War Two and we try to avoid violence now. As a nation."

"And, of course, the corrida is a source of compensation."

"You put it very well."

"I see the point you are making."

"I have retired from banking."

I finished my beer.

"I understand."

I rose and held out my hand. He rose, took my hand, and bowed.

"I wish you good luck," he said.

I did not have to return the wish. They had permitted him to retire, no doubt with a handsome bonus. They had asked him to come to me to suggest the benefits of cooperation—or mere passivity in the face of a gigantic mechanism that with the press of a finger of some functionary within it could turn briefly deadly by arranging some kind of fatal accident. They did not want to kill anyone directly. That was a weakness within an organization that probably killed thousands daily by indirection.

Who knows—perhaps they will hire me to deliver messages, as Senor Telefilo the retired banker had done. A new career beckoned.

Now I had the damned rest of the afternoon.

Just off the Paseo Colon, down a tiny street called Mariana Pineda, a cul de sac narrows to a dark and unpromising alley. One imagines at least one cutthroat in the shadows even at noon. But the alley opens onto a courtyard with a bountiful fountain that leaps to the sun then rumbles into shadow, and a sequence of tropical leaves that move westward on the air coming from the Guadalquivir. Under a wooden roof, lurks a tiled bar called El

Gallo with a single barman—a thin, darkeyed and silent Sevillano in a starched white shirt—who served me many beers that afternoon. I was the only one there. I made sure to taste each swallow of the beer. I ate olives and fresh, crusty bread on which I poured olive oil. Two men in suits looked into the patio, but left when they saw me. Perhaps, though, they just glanced in and went out again. Perhaps I was not the reason they left. I watched the evidence of a thunderstorm pock against the stones of the courtyard and turn the aspiring fountain into a hunchback. I could hear the sky and thought I could listen to the clouds twisting in a clockwise motion into an afternoon elsewhere, as the day cleared for the moment of the procession of the matadors, banderilleros, and picadors into the Maestranza.

I sit on my cushion—imported from Mexico, with Enrique Ponce's name on it. This is to make me look like an international aficionado to anyone who looks at the white names of Ponce, Cavazos, and Jorge Guitierrez inscribed on the purple canvas. The vendor goes by—"cerveza, cokecola, wikky." The whiskey, for some reason, is Cutty Sark. It is cloudy and the low sky holds a miasma of smoke. An old man rakes the sand with the patient absorption of a peasant as Manuel Cabellero in his golden suit, dances past to accept an ovation. His wolfish grin says, Look what you and I are doing together! His crowd is a collaborator in his brilliance. Abellan and Juli—two boys—are competing against each other. The crowd is judge. I am watching two versions of corrida here. Cabellero kicks his cape, like a debutant preparing to descend the staircase. The lights go on and now the suits of the matadors absorb its artificial glitter. I feel someone looking at me. Perhaps that man to my right? Perhaps, but it is Marie, glancing up for a moment from the callejon. Some rain skims from the clouds and, on the other side, comes a kind of moan and umbrellas thump open—the low level parachute jump of mourners.

    The rain begins to slither down on my side of the ring. Mercedes opens her umbrella and holds it over my head.

"Thanks," I say.

I see Marie glance up at me again. She smiles. So happy you are keeping your baldspot dry! She is wearing an Expos hat. She turns to take photographs.

The sand grows heavy, and Cabellero doffs his shoes. The bull skids. The storm rumbles off to Murcia, leaving a shelf of blue slate under the moon.

"A little bleary-eyed," Marie said later, as we had drinks at the Colon.

"Who, me? It is the price one pays for sheer concentration. And a few cervezas this afternoon. That little bar where the fountain is."

"An oasis in the middle of the madding crowd. Take me next time."

"It was your nap time."

I did not tell her about the discrete Spanish warning that the retired banker, Senor Telefilo, has come all the way from Malaga to deliver to me.

"To us," I said, touching my glass of beer to her glass of white wine.

We were sitting in the Egana Oriza, near my hotel, under huge windows with red and blue chevrons of stained glass running along large windows that looked out upon a lighted garden. The windows and the lights in the garden were cannily contrived to make the trees seem to move out for miles from this lighted place, so that it seems as if we were on the edge of a jungle. Someone has told Marie about the partridge marinated in sherry vinegar.

"How long do they cook it?" I asked, lifting a savory chunk toward my lips and letting the garlic swim the air to my nostrils.

"I would imagine they fry the partridge, add the rest, and cook it for about an hour and a half."

"They knew we were coming."

"They knew someone was. Want me to try it at home?"

Home—I paused for a moment and considered the concept.

"Yes."

"That is, assuming we get out of this alive."

I signaled our waiter for another round of drinks.

"Quisiera vino, cerveza, y un aguardiante, por favor"

"Make that two brandies," Marie said.

One of the men—the one who looked French, or perhaps Belgian—that Marie had photographed was staying at the Alfonso XIII. I saw him in the Loewe's shop to the right of the lobby as I came in from a visit to the Inglaterra one morning. He was holding an alligator case.

I waited and, by asking for my key at the same as he did, I was able to find that he was in suite 514. The next morning, I saw him leave his key at the desk. He did not have his alligator case with him. I got that feeling I get when I am out shopping—a rare thing for me to be doing—and see something I cannot afford but know I am going to buy. I think it must be what compulsive gamblers feel, or alcoholics as they contemplate their first drink of the day. It involves a barely palpable trembling and a light sweat. It's bad, it's exciting, it's inevitable.

The chambermaids were in Suite 511. I could never figure out the order in which rooms were made up, but I assumed that they had not been in the direction of 514 on the inside of the hallway looking down on the balcony that ran around the inner courtyard. I walked down the hallway and turned to make sure I knew which was the recessed entry to 514 down the long, redundant perspective of shadow and blue tile.

I waited at a corner of the empty corridor, peeking around to watch the chambermaids. If someone came along, of course, I'd have to walk in the other direction to the elevator and abandon my mission.

At last the cart full of towels, room service menus, and amenities pulled up at 514.

I walked down the corridor and turned into the entrance.

I waved my key at the women in the room.

"Hola! Buenas dias! Algo que yo olivido. I forgot something."

The case was closed, on a table. It was locked, but when all the numbers are put on zero it snaps open.

Passport. Baptiste Levesque. Canadian! That was a master stroke! Who would have suspected that a French Canadian was in on this huge scheme? Traveler's checks. And the memo. Two pages, both sides.

I went out of the room again. It would be close! Down to the second floor where the hotel offices were. Quickly, by way of the stairs.

"Xerox?" I said, smiling and holding up the two pages.

Hurry, hurry, I said to myself. Why wasn't I one of those secret agents who could photograph a page with his eyes?

"No rush," I said to the dark-haired woman.

"A guest?"

"Si. Habitacion 210," I said, holding up my magic key.

I might do better by imitating an important man in a hurry.

"Cuanto antes," I said. "As soon as possible."

"Por supuesto, senor!"

Back up those giant marble stairs—why do they show me what terrible shape I'm in?. My sweat was slick now, my breath short. I had wished the chambermaids to hurry only moments ago. Now, I prayed that they would slow up, take a break for a cuppa!

One woman was outside the room now, beginning to push the cart down the hallway. Don't shut the door!

"Again!" I said to the other one, just pulling the door closed. "Que dia!"

I put the memo back into the case, closed it, and rolled the tumblers again, wondering whether Levesque had memorized the previous setting. No. Clearly, he was not that careful—his habits were those of the business man, not of a professional crook or an international spy.

"Gracias! Gracias!"

I give each of the women a five thousand peseta note. I calculated the amount as too much for my brief intrusion on their bedmaking and vacuuming but enough to make them anticipate much more when the occupant of 514 left and thus enough to keep them quiet in the meantime. I hoped that Levesque was a good tipper.

I went back to my room, unfolded my xerox copies, and read my death warrant.

"They know we are watching," Don Alvaro said.

We sat on a patio on the shady side of the house, looking over a sandy stretch of scrubland down toward the copper thread of river. There, where the lush grass was, in the shadows of a grove of oak trees, lurked the black shapes of fighting bulls. Even from this distance, the brown pools of their eyes seemed to reflect us. Occasionally, a horn would flash across a moment of sunlight as the river wind shrugged against the trees.

"Very peaceful when they are together," he said. "Unlike men."

He swept his arm around the horizon, now beginning to heat with the day.

"A small ranch. 6000 hectares. That's about 15000 acres. The taxes on this land to support the urban way of life are enormous. The pressure to turn the land into ugly concrete is huge. Bulls are a hobby. A passion, but a hobby. I could not support this place with the bulls. I would have to sell off this or that section for housing estates. I have liquors. I own a good share of the Victoria brewery in Malaga. I export sherry—only the best—from Jerez and olive oil from Antequera. I am a principal in several banks—not large ones, but they don't have to be these days, do they? My grandfather would be appalled. For him it was the bulls and only the bulls. Of course the great matadors fought our bulls in those days."

His eyes grew opaque for a moment, as if he were looking at a ranch rolling out under the sky of seventy years before.

"They will move when they think they are going to be fed. And they do think. We feed them up here, of course—all the approved grains and supplements—because they have to come up the hill to eat. The ranch is only just big enough for the exercise. They need legs to run and bones and muscles to lift the horses and lungs for the last act. Some bulls nowadays are being raised in back yards. They fall down when the wind blows."

He snorted with contempt.

"They are on their knees before the sword goes in. Not these."

I had heard of the Pagano bulls, but never seen them.

"No one will fight them, of course," Don Alvaro said. "And no one demands that they do. I take them occasionally to Madrid or Bilbao."

"Why only there?"

"They don't shave the horns there."

"And you won't let your bulls be shaved."

"Never. Nunca."

He said this quietly, as a matter of fact.

I had seen the shaving of horns in Sevilla, of course, and I knew that Pagano bulls fought there from time to time. I said nothing. He could not help but know what happened in Sevilla.

"I have 120 cows. I can keep track of them. That's the blood line. I alter the semen line every third generation. Otherwise, we get those genetic problems—weak legs, bad lungs—that you see in so many plazas these days. You must hybridize, and it's too expensive for some of them."

He stared at the end of his cigar.

"They are business men, after all."

"How many bulls do you get from 120 cows?"

"Enough to keep my packing plant happy. Every five year cycle, perhaps enough for 3 or 4 encierros."

"About 20 to 24 bulls."

"Yes. The substitute bull is always from a different ranch. I send only six bulls to any given corrida. Look at it this way, Senor Kane. When I breed my best cow and my most reliable seed bull, I can still lose 50% of the positive genetic material. Of course . . ."

He paused to relight his cigar.

"I am producing what the demand is—if you can call it that. I would hate to send a good fighting bull straight to the slaughter house. His way to death must be through the bullring."

He gazed out across his acreage, then turned to look at me.

"Sevilla? You are thinking of Sevilla?"

"I was, yes," I said.

"They get an extra twenty percent to fight them there."

"I did not know that. I knew that it was true of the Miuras."

"Few people even know that much. The matadors do not want anyone to know. That I do is enough. If the Sevillianos knew they'd be even angrier than they are when those prima donnas go out, double the bull a couple of times, then stab it in the lungs. It robs the bull of the moment he has been born to have."

The matador has grown cynical enough to march out through a barrage of cushions and jeers to collect his check, knowing there will be easier bulls and triumphs ahead in other rings.

"Your bulls die with the horns in tact. I am glad to know that."

He looked at me again, his green eyes skeptical within their folds.

"Why are you here?"

If I lied, I would be politely shown to the door.

"To talk to you, Don Alvaro."

"Yes. I mean in Spain."

"Officially, I am studying the animal question. In reality . . . I don't know."

He nodded.

"Yes. You can say that my grandfather helped invent the peto. In the late 20s."

The peto is the protective padding—like a gym mat—that goes around the picadors' horses.

"I did not know that."

"A little history. To make your report seem authentic."

Was he mocking me?

"My grandfather, Primo de Rivera, and the American matador, Sidney Franklin."

Franklin was known as "the bullfighter from Brooklyn."

"Before that, the picadors of the matador whose bull was coming out were in the ring, under the president's box. They did not start coming out as a separate event until about 1929. It was strictly what you Americans would call cosmetic. The horses still suffered, though it was broken ribs, not wounds, cornadas."

"And the matadors approve."

He looked at me with sudden respect.

"Yes. The bull that has killed something is much more dangerous than the one who is merely frustrated. And the peto tires the bull."

I had driven to Ronda in a car I rented at the airport in Sevilla. By pulling many strings and slipping many 5000 peseta notes to many eager palms, I had set up a brief appointment with Don Alvaro Pagano. I had been told that he was the man Diogenes had been searching for with that failing lantern.

"Put in something about the transport," he said. "Some ranches send their deformed bulls and novillos in boxes to the provincial rings. Sometimes the trucks sit outside the corral for hours. Sometimes the animals suffocate. Seldom are they able to fight. They come into the sun from hours of heat and blackness. It is a wonder that they don't kill more men than they do. But they are already half-dead themselves. Put that in your report. No one will deny it, and, if you are pressed, I will give you a source you can cite. I do not like the way they treat the animals. That will sound strange to you?"

"No, it does not."

"The animal has a steel spike driven into its tossing muscle, sharp barbs into its shoulders, then the length of a sword through its aorta. But it never loses its nobility. If you treat it like veal, though . . ."

He shrugged, contemplated his cigar, and turned to me.

"But you know that already. What have you learned that is not about the bulls?"

I wondered whether he had heard of my being in that bank in Malaga. No. He could read my preoccupation, a nagging something working beneath my interest in his ranch and his bulls.

I told him some of what I had surmised. I did not tell him about the memo I had copied. It was simply fear I think, that kept me from telling him that. I trusted him, but the words themselves seemed dangerous as I scrolled them in my mind.

"This has always been a land of rich and poor. I have always been among the former group, even if we were never rich. But we took care of our workers. Gave their wives a doctor or a midwife for their childbirths, buried them with a priest we paid and in ground we gave them and with a stone we had carved for them. Now, it is a land of greed. I have seen what aid can do. When we let the Americans in in the 60s—well, you see our roads and our electricity now. Now, the money does not go where it should go. It sticks to the fingers of those greedy bastards. People still hate Franco, but say what you will about him, Franco made sure the money went where it was supposed to go. Say what you will about him, Spain was first in his heart. The king, too."

"You know him?"

"Well enough to call him anytime I have something to say to him."

He laughed his dry, inward laugh.

"Would he ever do anything?"

"He? No."

"He wouldn't"

"He would let things be known. But about this? Nothing can be proved, Senor Kane."

He rose and tossed his cigar into the sand beyond the patio.

"You see those stones up there?"

He pointed at a row of headstones glinting now in the full reach of the morning. "It is a comfort to know that I will be there. I am in no hurry, but there are my father, his father, and his father before him. And the wives, too, Senor Kane, the ones from whom the courage comes. Believe me, when I say that. My own wife is there. And Paulino Ruiz."

"Paulino Ruiz?"

"You have heard of him?"

"A matador killed in the ring at Las Ventas. His first bull there."

"You have done your reading. Yes. His last bull there. He said, in the infirmary, 'Bury me where the bulls are.' Not all matadors are aficionados, you know, just as many athletes know nothing about the game they play. You see why I want to keep this place and raise bulls here. You know, Sr. Kane, there are days when I realize suddenly that I am old. Almost 70. I don't realize that most of the time. I feel my skin, like paper against the razor in the morning. Then I think. What has changed. I will tell you. Men no longer dream. That is not just an old man without dreams talking. Look at the world today. Greed and disease. That is it. Greed and disease. Yes. The sun will be coming around this corner and bringing Africa with it. Let us go inside. I assume that you, like most North Americans would not refuse a beer?"

"I start getting thirsty at noon, Don Alvaro."

We went into a cool and dark-paneled room. Under the indirect lighting were the heads of many bulls, staring glassily into the shadows, having lost that alertness that crystallizes in the eyes of fighting bulls in the sun of the plaza de toros. If you are close enough, you see that intelligence and the danger. Below them, in thin wooden frames, were posters, bright still these many years later. Guerrita, Largajito, Joselito, Belmonte, Gaona, Granero, Manera, La Landa, El Estudiante, Ortega, and underneath the names of the matadors was the legend "Con Toros de Pagano."

Don Alvaro spoke into space in the wall that looked like the front of an old radio. Almost instantly, a woman in a black dress and white apron brought me a beer, Don Alvaro a brandy.

I looked at the posters and sipped my beer. I felt time rolling backward to July of 1912 where we could have taken a carriage from the Hotel No Hay Presupuesto to the bullring of Valencia and seen Fuentes, Bombita, Gallito, and Vincente Pastor with bulls of Miura, The Duke of Veragua, Pablo Romero, and Don Augustine Pagano. I felt the ink on these dry old posters in their thin black frames damp again from the printers, the blood on the backs of the bulls pulsing out again into the sand, the blood of the matador darkening the gold brocade of his suit of lights. For an instant I was back in his grandfather's time, in the great moment when Don Augustine lived only for his bulls.

One poster for Las Ventas, the ring of Mardrid, for 18 April 1941 listed Pascal Marquez with bulls of Concha y Sierra.

"The wind blew his muleta against his body," I said. "The bull ripped his ribcage out, exposing his heart."

"They kept him alive for almost two weeks. Today, who knows?"

He shrugged his shoulders.

"You are an aficionado," Don Alvaro said, quietly.

"No. Interested, though."

"It is aficion. One feels it. Rare,"

"Among the blue-eyed devils?"

He laughed.

"Even among us. Many go for social reasons. You have noticed that they dress up and are seen. It is an event. But a few go for the bulls."

"If so, it sneaked up on me."

"It is usually a moment."

And it had been a moment—when the horns went past Abellan's right leg as he performed a gaonera and I felt time stop for that moment. I had also see the brightness of the horn for an instant before it entered the shade.

"It was a moment," I said. "Literally an epiphany."

I described it to him. We were sitting in leather chairs. A thin slice of late morning came through the shutters and made a sword across the oaken table between us. The splinter of light was full of dust.

"Look, Lorenzo. Get out of this country. There is danger here for you. Write your report and forget all about what you have heard, and about what you suspect. Let me tell you, nothing can be done. Nothing will be done. No evidence exists, for one thing. For another, anyone voicing any suspicions, anyone suspected of being suspicious, will simply disappear. A stone thrown into a river. I know enough to want to know no more. Call it what you will. I am interested in keeping this ranch for my son. And he will keep it for his. They can buy officials like bales of hay, even if the price of hay is going up. Take my advice. Get away while you can. Otra cerveza?"

"No thank you. I want to have a look at Ronda."

"Be careful. You have enough for your report?"

I laughed.

"More than enough, Don Alvaro."

"Cuidado, Lorenzo. Please come back to Spain. I would like you to see my bulls in the ring."

Ronda had been built high on top of a gorge and had been a defensive position and observation post for several armies over several centuries. I walked across the narrow bridge that separated the two sections of the city, but did not pause to look down into the valley far below. I was not afraid, exactly, but I had the sense of being observed. I walked to the bullring, the oldest in Spain, they claim, dating from 1785 and little changed since then. Instead of the wooden strip that runs around the inside of the ring—so the banderilleros can leap the fence when the bull chases them—Ronda retained its original stone. In front of the ring were bronze statues of Caetanyo Ordonez—Nino de la Palma, the model for Hemingway's matador in *The Sun Also Rises*—and his great son Antonio Ordonez., the young bullfighter who gets the better of Luis Miguel Dominguin in Hemingway's *The Dangerous Summer*. It was from the heights of Ronda that Hemingway's Pablo had walked the local landowners in *For Whom the Bell Tolls*. Time rolled back again and I thought of being there when Hemingway was young and writing so well of Spain in clean, well-lighted capitols of the world. He was no doubt a cocky, drunken son-of-a-bitch, but I would have liked to hear that prose for the first time. I would not have wished to be there at the end, when all that was left was ego and alcohol. And despair. I stood in the empty sand of the ring and imagined the crunch of a bull's hooves. Would I be able to stand still? No. We are afraid of different things at different times of our lives.

I leaned against the rough stones of the bridge. The shell of a house sat on a ledge halfway down, between the clenched ribs of the cliff and the miniature valley. Why the house had been abandoned to erode to its staring skull was obvious. How it had gotten there was not.

As I drove down the side of the mountain again, I asked myself whether Don Alvaro had been told to warn me. No, I thought. He knew. He was not one of the cabal of greed that Marie and I had stumbled on to at their meeting in Sevilla. He was old Spain. His name meant "Pagan," so that he might even have come of a distant Roman family Christianized in the 4th century. Maybe I am beginning to think at last, I said to myself, laughing. Yes, I thought, I should get away. I would. take Marie and I would leave soon. But "soon" is not good thinking in an emergency. I felt something coming down the mountainside behind me, something big and fast that would brush me over the guard rail and down the rocky wall. And even as I trembled with imaginary terror between the shoulders of the mountains, I felt the country taking over. I wanted to leave. And, I knew, as soon as I left, I would want to come back.

I thought of the empty plaza de toros, behind me on the plateau. The ancient ring at Ronda cuts the light in half at six o'clock. To that semi-circle the bull is brought to where the horse purples its shoulders, as the pic probes colors of the night, and blood streams down the flanks of the black bull, who wheels to the rebolera's twist, to drive a horn into the sun, his heart alive, pulsing, as the matador crosses for the kill. The road back sidles down the mountain. Beyond, the many more rise purple with the sun, which subdivides the valley floor, the land filled with a curving of olive trees where run the streams. The road curls up to the diamond of a star. A black shape looms where light is done.

I thought of Don Alvaro, indignant at the treatment of animals that have been bred to be killed in giant rings like Las Ventas in Madrid or in circles formed by the tipping over of farmer's carts in the stony heat of village squares. I would include his indignation in my report and add "Source Available Upon Request," knowing that no one would dispute the description of fighting bulls suffocating as the scalding gaze of a Spanish August withered the boards of the trucks.

I was anxious to see Marie. I had left her in Sevilla, getting some of her pictures developed at a local newspaper, where she had befriended the photographer of toros. It is, I thought, the purple light of a summer's night in Spain, as Cole Porter has it. Few countries can contrast their nights and days as Spain can. The white villages of Andalucia spill from the shoulders of the mountains. The fortress stone is strewn nearby and takes the light like bone, like the soldiers of long ago, called up to fill the parapets, define the frontier between two ways of talking about God. And so they fight, blindly debating another source of sight, where blood has been pulled away by soil or stream. The light balances between the mountainsides. A moonman comes up and begins to watch the rim of a world on the other side. Gray-faced, he rides on purple shoulders and rises to brush the unseen memory across his eyes. He bides the time and searches where the sun has been.

I now rode the long valley toward the distant twist of light that is the city. Once, I thought, people cared enough about God— or, like the Medici popes, about the profitable position they had taken in relationship to God—to kill, even to die for those beliefs. Martyrs did exist. Thomas Beckett, Cranmer, More. Now, it was either, how did I get my hands into that pile of gold? or how do I live according to who I think I am and am supposed to be? Don Alvaro was one of the latter. Marie didn't even have to think about it. I? Could I walk away from what I was beginning to learn about the group that had hired Roger Baldwin and killed him? It was not revenge for Baldwin. I wish I could say that it was a wish to do the right thing. As I rolled into Sevilla and tried to figure out where I was, so that I did not have to drive through too many sidewalk restaurants, I knew it was curiosity. A small voice talked about what had killed many cats. It said, get out! Get out now! That is now as in whenever the next flight takes off for anywhere from the airport. Grab Marie and get the hell out!

The restaurant called Casa Blanca was at the end of a smoky bar in an ungainly alley where two sections of the city had met two hundred years ago just beyond the Plaza Nuevo. The restaurant guaranteed that you could eat the meat of the bulls killed just hours before in La Maestranza and carted from the side entrance of the Plaza by the trucks of Senor Munoz, Purveyor of the Meat of Fighting Bulls. Carne de los toros de la Plaza!

"Man is looking at you," Marie said.

"At you. Want me to go punch him?"

"No. Save what's left of your nose, dear one. He's looking at you."

"He has to look somewhere."

"He understands English."

"Some people do."

On the pretext of summoning more wine from our waiter, I glanced at the man.

I had seen him before. Where? The associations were pleasant, but I could not recall the circumstances.

Marie's eyes rose as the man stood and crossed the three or four steps to our table.

"Senor Kane, I do not wish to interrupt you, but I wanted to tell you how much I liked your *Aeneid*. I saw it in New York."

I half rose and shook his hand.

He went back to his table.

"Paranoid," I whispered to Marie.

"I keep forgetting that I am with a famous person. But you are the one who is reading shadows these days."

"That's true. But there's a reason."

I told her what I had overheard at the bank in Malaga. I had hoped to avoid that, since it stank of danger, but Marie was part of this.

She replied as softly as I had narrated my story.

"We've know there's something fishy about what we were doing. How does it fit in with what you overheard? Does it?"

"Oh, yes. Don Alvaro made that clear enough."

I told her about the memo I had copied, and tucked under the green cardboard in the writing pad in my room. It was something a searcher would lift up to look under.

"The scope of the thing is breathtaking! We knew that we were doing something completely different that what we were really doing. Like an allegory."

"An allegory? I suppose so. Every detail on the surface has a single deeper meaning."

"But the meanings are disjunctive."

"As in a cover story."

"Yes," she said. "We are part of the cover story. Imagine the trouble they are gong to . . ."

I put my finger to my lips.

"Yes," she said. "And imagine the money they are spending just on setting up an opposite set of signals."

"Malaga explains it. The money they spend on us is nothing compared to what they are taking in."

"Let's get out of here."

"Okay. Let me finish my wine."

"I mean Spain."

"We will. Soon. I've still got a couple of things to do."

"I've got all the pictures I need."

"Day after the day after tomorrow."

"I don't know," she said. "That sounds like never."

It was afternoon and it was raining. I suddenly realized that I would be disappointed if I did not see Enrique Ponce that day in the bullring. He was Numero Uno in Spain. Well, Marie and I would find something else to do. I sat there and listened to the storm.

The thunder rumbles with a Spanish voice, because it echoes from the river banks clotted with Bouganvellia to the ranks of cloud ribbed like skeletons. The noise of storm mutters in the patio. Will there be bulls tonight? And will the sword summon one more time the holy word—torero? The swing of Abellan's gaonera—this stopped the moment for a sunglint, low horn thirsting for the negligent leg, the hiss of blackness past, the dark and muscular flow, the still, golden man, the passing of the wish of the beast to find the bone and roar muerto!

I got up from my chair by the window, went over to the writing pad on the desk, retrieved my copy of the memo, and sat down and read it again.

Working notes. YOUR EYES ONLY.

I have no choice but to preside over the World Hunger Forum, and, unless the Inner Council meets now, we can't pull an IC session together for a month or so. So here are the primary points to reemphasize. The main thing is—we want ideas from them. Nothing that I list briefly below will be news to them, but it will pumpprime some ideas. No recording. No notetaking. Recheck security with Copeland. You will write a memo for me—one copy only. Destroy this memo immediately after the meeting. I will be at the Savoy (0171 836 4343), but do not call, fax, or e-mail me unless it is a code 5 emergency.

Encourage the individuals to come up with catch phrases. Those you *can* record. Remind the group how successful we were in 1990 with "If we don't deal with him now, we'll be dealing with him five years down the road," and, among students, "If I saw a rape occurring on campus, of course I would take action." The evidence strongly suggests that the action taken is to ignore the rape, but people like to have clichés at their command which they can utter as if original thought and considered conviction. I am sure the group can improve on the samples I include below.

Support free trade with China. Mythology is that free trade will "open up" China, encourage reforms in human rights. Since corporations are more authoritarian than China's government, such changes are strongly counterindicated. But opening trade relations also opens channels for the flow of money in and out of Chinese financial institutions. It will be to our advantage to open up a vast new field of cheap labor in China, though no one seems to recognize that "job creation" there will be one of the immediate results of China's entrance into world markets. On this one, money to US politicians unlimited. "Free Trade Is Good for Farmers." Some farmers may actually swallow that, even if it tastes like a soybean burger.

It should be noted re China that our orchestration of the bombing of the Chinese Embassy in Belgrade in 1999 was a mistake. Our calculus suggests that controlling the CIA at this point in time is not as vital to our interests as opening China. We have the CIA anyway. Where else can they go? "We Need Intelligence!"

Celebrate "democracy" when a former Coca Cola executive is elected as a result of the "democratic process." It simply means that we have a different group of people to talk with. In the case of Mexico, of course, the results can be made to seem to be attributable to NAFTA. "Free Trade Means Democracy."

Continue to support Reagan's "Starwars" programme with the politicians who do not want to be perceived as "weak on U.S. defense." It is a great drainer of money that would otherwise be wasted on social programs and education into a scheme that will never work. It is globally destabilizing, particularly with a power like China and with Russia, still smarting from its great fall. Debate about it is another splendid diversion on our diversionary chessboard.

Furthermore, we might make inroads with one of those "rogue nations" we have invented and thus wield unusual power at some moment as yet unborn. I like the way we have linked the programme to the mundane activity of raising an umbrella. "In Case It Rains!"

Continue to endorse schemes like the U.S. cropdusting of poppy fields in Columbia. This approach has laid waste to vast stretches of arable land and thus opens up need for "developmental programmes" like ours. Don't permit people to grasp the fact that we are supporting a corrupt regime. Cocaine and heroin production has doubled in Columbia since 1995. "Stamp Out Drugs at Their Source."

Support U.S. intervention in the domestic disputes of foreign countries. That may be a lost cause, of course, and we'll never have another situation as wide-open as Vietnam was (unless it is going to be in Columbia), but there is no underestimating the stupidity of U.S. elected and appointed officials. "Vietnam Was Not in Vain"—but we say that only through the voices of our revisionist friends of the far right. They think the Iron Curtain is still in place. Encourage that fiction.

Continue to fund protests in major cities. Seattle. D.C. Brussels. The more objections to our overt goals, particularly as "capitalistic," the more we are put in the easy rhetorical position of defending those goals. The weaker our position is perceived to be, the better. That weakness fuels the irrelevant debate about who we are and what we are trying to do which obscures both who we are and what we are doing. "Down with Global Greed."

Promote "computer literacy" and computer availability in schools. Let people move all the information they want. We move money. "Computer Literacy Is Empowering."

Continue to support—with funds to legislators at all levels and to metropolitan police departments, where needed—the "War on Drugs" in the United States. It means far less surveillance of large banking transactions like ours, which are not drug-related, and suppresses civil rights to an extent few U.S. citizens have noticed. They "support" it. Keep fees high for Bennett, McCaffrey, et al to promote "War on Drugs." Fight notion in columns and "op ed" pieces that drugs keep certain segment of population pacified, or killing each other, or in penal institutions. If true intention of "War on Drugs" is realized, protests against it could escalate beyond a few eastern and far-western universities. "One War We *Can* Win."

Encourage investigations of individual corporations—Archer, Daniels, Midland, Microsoft, Sprint, etc. Looking into their fraud or their monopolistic tendencies pulls the governments away from detecting where the real linkages are. Keep them examining the wrong structures. "Business is Not Monkey Business." Keep funding ads calling for corporate honesty and concern for the public interest.

Continue pseudo-security crises in U.S.—atomic secrets and that sort of thing. Pay big bucks. Diversion is remarkably useful. "Protect U.S. Security." "PUS"—that has a nice resonance!

Sponsor pseudo-events like marrying millionaires, and promote scandals in the private lives of government officials. If we keep the media busy with them, they have no time or wish to look at real issues. "All Play and No Work—the Way It Should Be" or "No One Is Above the Law," depending on the circumstances.

When in doubt—and most candidates try not to commit to anything specific—money goes to Republican, conservative, Tory candidates on all levels. Their constituencies are likely to support our policies, even if an occasional candidate turns out to be a maverick. "It's Your Vote—Make It Count!"

A Republican President in the U.S. will appoint judges who will rule consistently against all regulation of business. That tendency is obviously to our advantage. "Free Enterprise Must Be Free of Government Bureaucracy!"

Encourage purchase of public lands—especially in US by private corporations. We will get our share of every transaction and of the sale of products (oil, timber, minerals) from those lands. It is much easier for us to place a man on the board of one of those corporations than to submit him to the Congressional confirmation process for a cabinet position. "It's Your Land, Not the Government's!"

Support efforts of organized labor in the U.S. for higher wages and better benefits packages. Higher wages force industries to look elsewhere for their workers. A movement of manufacturing to countries with cheap labor will create splendid opportunities for our loan mechanisms. "Unions—Backbone of American Industry."

Encourage market mergers, like that of the London and Frankfurt exchanges. Get them to quarrel over whether to use pounds or eurodollars. The more confusion the better, and we thrive in a murky regulatory environment. "Big Money Makes For Bigger Markets."

Let reformers believe that, though we don't have J. Edgar or the CIA in our pocket anymore, we can get anyone who looks like an enemy, and we can control the aftermath. Let them believe that that includes two Kennedys and one King. It should still stun people that they got one—one!—murderer for each hit. "Our Arm Is Long"—but only use that when other modes of negotiation have failed.

Support futile UN "peace keeping" in African countries. The more unrest, the more refugees, the more "permanent camps," the more hostage taking, the more hunger and famine, the more the "need" for our humanitarian operations. The more instability within governments, the easier to conceal the flow in and out of our money. The weak and piecemeal UN approach exacerbates the problems of these "emerging nations" and prolongs their duration. "Peaceful Solutions to Conflict."

Continue support for groups focussed on the "environment," and for politicians actively, if covertly, fighting them. The debate is a splendid diversion. The more violent the better. The burning of police cars invariably creates vivid images on the news programmes. "We Breathe the Same Air."

Support education about "AIDS" in sub-Sahara Africa, but not the introduction of drugs and clinics, as some UN functionaries have proposed. Once population is suitably decimated—3 or 4 years?—we can begin what will prove to be a very profitable chemical program there. Say we are studying with great interest the Bristol-Myers-Squibb and Gates-World Health Organization initiatives. Right now, we ourselves don't want some smartass from the UN looking over our shoulder. "Against Insidious DiseaseS."

Support "cultural literacy" program throughout Africa and Asia, some countries in Central and South America. They buy the texts from Rico Publications. We make 75% on each book purchased, even if they rot in the rain once they're delivered. "The Truth Will Make You Free."

Support Japan's tight money policies. They really do think that technology alone is going to create a huge boom for them. They still dream of the days when they exported all those cars and stereos. They apparently cannot see that their monetary policies are driving them into a deep recession. Soon they will need our own set of programs, designed for the "second-tier" countries who are no longer the most powerful players in the global economy. Japan!

It will be a gold mine for us. Scrap "A Yen for the Yen." We cannot use "Remember Pearl Harbor." "Ride the Wave of E-Commerce!" It is about to crash on top of them.

Remember—governments are short-lived. The cabinet minister we talk with today may be executed next week. Governments will want concrete proof of the value of their policies—good works like roads, schools, and dams. We will give them enough of these things to satisfy the public relations aspect of our enterprise. Governments do not analyze process. As long as we control the process, we control the flow of money. "Tangible Evidence of Progress!"

Remember—we want their ideas. As they know, money is not an issue. Any ideas they float will be balanced against the cost ratio, anyway, so encourage brainstorming. "Today—the World!" Remind them that it is easy to get the money. It is not as easy to move it. It is difficult to hide it and at the same time have access to it. We have to be creative when it comes to the problems we face.

Make sure that all members are met quietly at the airport. NO SIGNS WITH NAMES ON THEM. We have three protocol officers assigned and a separate checkpoint at customs, to the left of the EU booths. Four limos have been laid on to shuttle back and forth from the airport to this site. Those limos will be waiting just outside of customs. Each will have a discrete blue and gold logo on the right front door. Copeland will be there with a checklist.

It still read like a death warrant. I hid it again beneath the blotter on the desk.

We were in El Cairo, a bustling place on the Reyes Catolicos just off the Paseo Colon, a few blocks above the bullring. It was close to Marie's hotel, and I intended to spend some time there—until at least dawn—once we had consumed an opulent meal of probably dangerous shell fish, crispy sardines, and perfectly safe grilled salmon. The white wine was disappearing like water.

"I thought you said that Ponce always took the bull to where it wanted to fight."

"That's what I read."

"What happened then?"

Ponce had fought his second bull in its quarencia, where the horses had been, and where it could smell its own blood. Most matadors would lead the bull away from that place close to the fence and fight it nearer the center of the ring. Ponce's had been an unsatisfactory fight—only a few obligatory passes with the left hand some doubling passes with the right hand designed to get the bull's head down, and then he had decided to kill.

"Ponce knows his bulls," I said. "Either he wasn't interested—and I doubt that—this is Sevilla, after all. He has done well here only once—last September—or he decided that the bull would be more dangerous and even less tractable in another terrain. In September, they say, he took a bull over to the gate from which it had just left. It was where it wanted to be, and, apparently, where it wanted to fight. It was also where it was probably most dangerous. He got two ears. Anyway, I defer to his intelligence."

"Can you give up too soon?"

I had to think for a moment. Who did she mean?

"Some matadors do. You can see them doing it, saying, no one can fight this beast. So they don't try. Not Ponce."

"Disappointing, though."

"Have you become interested?"

"Haven't you."

"A question with a question. Yes, I have. I hate to leave Spain."

"We'll come back."

In the wash of voices flowing up from the first floor to the shadowy balcony where we sat looking out over the late night crowd on the sidewalk and street, with a good white wine perking along my veins, and the vision of Marie's dark hair and dark eyes and pale skin replicated in the window beside her like a portrait on an ancient piece of sheet music, I felt danger melting away, tension relaxing along my shoulders.

"Reminds me of that place in London."

"What place?"

"Sitting on the balcony."

"Sure. Paradiso e Inferno."

"Our first date. We still should be careful," she said.

"Right," I said, not listening to the word.

A man came up to the table and bowed.

"Senor Kane. I am Roderigo Pagano."

I stood and introduced him to Marie.

"Will you join us?"

"I am at another table, thank you. I know that you had a discussion with my father a day or so ago. I wanted to tell you that you have friends here, but also that people are watching you. I do not think that they are your friends. My own suggestion—and I do not like to intrude on anyone's affairs—is that you would be wise to leave Sevilla, you and your companion, as soon as possible. Good luck!"

He bowed and walked away, down the steps to the main dining room.

"People are certainly watching, friends or not," Marie said.

"He's a friend. He will be in charge of the Pagano Ranch one day."

But how to undercut a romantic mood, I thought.

Just as well. Romantic moods can set one up for deception—in romance, which was not my worry, but in other areas, which were my worry.

"I will leave you at your room," I said.

"I thought you were going to stay!"

"I was, but I had better get back to my place, put some things together, pack, get ready. We had better leave no later than Saturday."

"Is that too late?"

"Of course not. They are just watching me. If I rushed off, they might follow."

"I understand that, but it may be a matter of rushing. And I am part of this, don't forget."

"I haven't. I think we still have a few days, though."

I was wrong.

To observe the nature and quality of my being observed, and to continue my pose as aficionado of the bulls, I took a cab to the San Fernando Cemetery, northeast of the city. There is buried Joselito, the great matador killed by the little bull in Talavera in 1920, in a tomb under a massive sculpture of the many people of Spain carrying a coffin on their shoulders forever to the grave. Joselito's brother-in-law, Sanchez Mejias, also killed by a bull, is buried somewhere in the same tomb. Across from Joselito is the flamboyant figure of Paquirri, doing a fancy finishing pass known as a rebolera. He was gored in the provincial ring of Pozoblanco in 1984. He talked calmly for about a halfhour in the infirmary, paused to take a breath for another word, and had nothing more to say.

I stood under the nodding shadows of the palms and looked at the graves of these matadors. I'd have to ask where Belmonte was. Since he had not been killed by the bulls, but had put a bullet into his head, perhaps he was not in consecrated ground.

From behind Paquirri's eternal rebolera, I saw a head move.

I walked around the statue.

"Senor!"

A craggy face looked at me, deep lines and sandy skin, the color of the ring of the Maestranza.

I figured he was a broken down banderillero who hung around the tombs, looking for a handout, a couple of coins worth of change from buying flowers.

"Senor, I watch. You have been followed."

I turned toward the entrance of the cemetery.

"Two men, down where they sell the flowers."

Some old men in Spain simply watch. They wait for weeks and, every once in a while, they see something. This old banderillero—if that's what he was—used to put the sticks in to a precise spot, a foot and a half behind the bull's horns. Had he seen anything with those keen eyes gleaming from his folded face?

A large, circular flower shop just outside the gate was designed to make you feel guilty as you passed by without buying flowers for the dead. Perhaps here, in this Catholic country, they themselves were not beyond guilt, but burning in flames in some place only God could see.

I edged out from the replica of Paquirri. An old woman, all in black, scuffed toward the cemetery with a yellow and red tribute to the happiness of fifty years ago, or perhaps just to a different kind of pain. Beyond the old woman were two men. One was the man from the *sorteo*.

Could I just walk past them and hail a cab?

"Senor, if you want, I can show you another way."

Sure—why not disappear? I did not feel any danger here among the palm and orange trees in the orange sun of a Sevillian morning, but it would be fun to evaporate more or less in front of the eyes of those two guys. I should have let them take me wherever they wanted to take me, but I did not know that then.

We walked down a long avenue of tombs, deep into a replica of an age-old Sevilla, sad eyed virgins staring forever at the pathway, fewer flowers as we walked, until we were in a zone of rainstained gray tombs unvisited for fifty years. What is so different about this city within a city? I wondered. It is the silence.

Yes, this old man had the heel and toe step of the bullfighter. I guessed that he had had a real pigtail, too, not one of those phony clipons they use today. Now what hair he had was pulled back over a scalp the color of a dead fish on a lake bottom.

"This way."

A small gate led to a twisted street of blue-tiled buildings, towering after the miniature columns and the statuary of the squat temples of these inner avenues. Out there, the street rattled and clanked but did not intrude on the rivers of silence behind me.

"I get a cab."

He did. I gave him a 5000 peseta note.

"I was 'Pablito.'"

"I am honored, Pablito."

He might have been a great banderillero when Manolete and Ortega were fighting. I was Rita Hayworth. I was Ava Gardner. Perhaps little Pablo had been there that day in Linares, when the shaved right horn of Islero drove into the groin of Manolete.

I left him with his hand held up as if a montera were in it and he was holding the hat out to the salutes of the crowd in La Maestranza.

"Rio Grande," I said. "Triana."

I was meeting Marie for lunch. I suddenly shuddered. I had been close to a hundred thousand deaths, a hundred thousand epitaphs. Mine would be, "Well, anyway . . ." But not yet. We were getting the hell out of here.

III.

"You take a cab to the Inglaterra. I'll walk across to the Alfonso. Meet me at the coffee shop down on the right hand side of the airport."

"Where are we going?"

"There's a flight to Barcelona at four. We'll go there, get tickets for tomorrow, get a room at the Ritz, find a good restaurant . . ."

"I like that idea."

"Barcelona?"

"A room at the Ritz."

"Tired of sleeping alone?"

"The sleep is okay."

We were on the sidewalk, turning left on the Paseo Cuba toward the bridge from Triana to Sevilla. A greasy waft of the McDonald's on the other side rode across the river. A car stopped at the edge of the traffic circle. Two men came up on either side of us. I felt my right elbow clenched in powerful fingers. The doors of the car popped open on the sidewalk side.

"Get in, please. Entre ustedes! Immediatamente!"

Marie was in the back seat, between two men—one already there. I was in the front seat. The locks on the tan Mercedes clunked shut and the car was on its way. Two Spanish cops in white and blue checkerboard hats stared out over the rattle of the palm leaves and the hum of the traffic circling the Paseo.

The car turned right.

"You are in no danger," said one of the men in the back seat. I got a glimpse of him as the sun darted down between buildings. He was the Spaniard with bulging brown Picasso eyes and an elegant cream-colored suit. Today, the suit was gray silk.

"Are you police?" I asked.

"Don't worry about who we are. We must blindfold you for a short while. You must excuse me. Desculpame, por favor."

He put a blindfold around Marie. The other man in the back seat—it was he man who had taken the film from Marie—reached forward, tipped my chin back, and blindfolded me. The blindfold was cotton and smelled of an expensive cologne—Versace, perhaps. We were being kidnapped first class.

"What do you want to know? We are leaving Sevilla this afternoon."

"You are, Senor Kane, but not perhaps as you had planned. I am not the one to ask questions. I suggest that you do not either."

"But this is kidnapping."

"You asked if we were the police."

In which case, of course, it would be detention for interrogation, no doubt covered by a ream of stamped documents. But these gentlemen were not the police.

I felt the hollowness beneath us as we crossed the bridge opposite the bullring. We then turned left. It was like flying under the hood in instrument training. You lowered a canvas covering over your head so all you could see was the panel in front of you—airspeed, altimeter, rate-of-climb, artificial horizon, omni screen, and engine instruments. It was an invitation to vertigo.

Marie asked quickly in English, "Should I not feel well?"

"It's okay," I said. "We're okay as long as they still have questions to ask."

"You are wise, Senor," said the man to Marie's left, the Spaniard, obviously the leader of this expedition.

I felt the sun drift across the windshield as we turned on to a highway.

We were headed toward Cordoba.

"Cuidado, Curro. Slow down!" said the other man in the back seat. "This is no time to be pulled in by the policia de trafico."

The driver, Curro, muttered something under his breath.

"You want to drive?"

"I do not want to drive, Curro. We can get plenty of drivers."

"Si, Senor Comstock," said the driver, his voice saying that he was aware of the threat. But not as good a driver as I am, it implied. Still, I could hear in his voice the thought of his wife and children. Maria y los bambinos. Comstock was like Roger Baldwin. A bully. I did not, however, embrace the popular cliché that bullies are automatically cowards. A lot of bullies had real power and a just as real sadism.

A clever lad—Simon Templar, for example—would have had these hombres fighting in another thirty seconds.

As it was, talk subsided into the powerful hum of the engine.

Marie and I had been sitting in the Rio Grande.

The day was a mix of clouds and sky, so the river, not knowing what to do, was gray and trying to become green. Up the river, the circular façade of the Maestranza was breathing out the last whisps of cigar smoke from its white and mustard colored circles. Bougainvillea splashed down the steep slopes toward the water. The "Luna de Sevilla" lumbered out with a few tourists aboard. The Tower of Gold glittered in its wake, and the chimes of the Giralda shouldered across to touch Triana where we sat, she behind the steam of sword fish—"pez espada"—and I above the savory gravy of "Rabo de Toro"—the tail of one of the bulls killed last night at the Real Maestranza and delivered immediately to the neighbor restaurants by Munoz, Purveyors of the Meat of Fighting Bulls.

"You award yourself the tail," she said.

"Sometimes it is awarded, yes. I'm sure it tastes better than the ears. Only vegetarians can really object to bullfighting."

"The animals are killed anyway."

"Right, and these bulls have a great life until they are five."

She gazed across the river.

"Looks like a medieval city—if you sort of squint at that modern telecommunications building."

"They've got an ordinance. No highrises. In Malaga, you can barely see the bullring anymore. Sevilla looks almost as it did when the conquistadors brought those ships creaking to the gunwales with gold down the Gualdquivir. You have enough pictures?"

"Yeah. I got the bull who killed himself on the fence, and the one who tore his horn off. Plenty of horses down in the sand and being probed by the horns."

"You still have that roll?"

"Sure. Too bad you didn't get one of the horn shaving."

"That would have been a smart move. I think I would have been shaved. We have what we came for. Let's get out of here."

"Now?"

"As soon as we finish lunch, and the wine."

"You have a whole bottle left."

"Half."

"Why now? Why not the other night?"

"We're being followed. I am, at least. You get the rest of those pictures developed. I file my report. Then we take a vacation. I have a friend who lives on Maui. He keeps wanting me to come visit."

"Let's just stay in Maine," she had said.

I felt the car dip down hill and did the Valsalva Maneuver—the swallowing that equalizes the pressure in the ears. A view of Cordoba would have spread before my eyes had I been able to see.

I heard Curro mutter as a car hissed by in the fast lane. Curro was driving with exaggerated caution, perhaps hoping that Comstock would tell him to speed up. But Comstock was too smart to play games with Curro.

The car stopped at a light. We turned left across a bridge. I could feel the wind along the river probing the left side of the car. Curro drove into the city, stopping for lights, turning right, then left, then going up hill again. So—we were headed into the hills north of Cordoba—scrubby badlands, punctuated by an occasional field of sunflowers or an olive grove.

What did they think I knew? They must know that I had overheard the conversation in Malaga. Could I pretend that I hadn't understood a word? I could try. Why hadn't they grabbed me before this? Did they want Marie, or was she just unlucky enough to be with me when they decided to bring me in for questioning? They wanted both of us, obviously. Damn! I had to hope that they were bringing her along as a precaution, perhaps as something to use against me. If they didn't think she knew anything, she'd be safe for the time being. I didn't have to guess about who these guys were. How high up in the hierarchy they would turn out to be once we got to where we were going was another question. The Spaniard in the cream-colored suit was no underling. He must be their operations manager. What were they going to do with us? It could be that they would be able to prove that this was "official questioning" and let us go—but only if they thought we posed no threat. As it was, I had that position paper I'd copied hidden in my room at the Alfonso. It didn't prove a thing, of course, except that I knew the extent of their conspiracy. So—it was my death warrant if they found it. In other words, we still had a chance here, particularly if we were going to meet one or more of the big boys. What chance we had lay in my ability to play dumb. I'd done it well for most of my life, but it's hard when you're trying, tricky when it is not just an unconscious reflex of natural behavior. Damn! I thought—if only I had let them capture me outside the cemetery! My exciting escape had only gotten Marie into this mess.

I knew now what that trip to the place where they shaved the horns had meant. It had been a warning, delivered in the indirect Spanish way. The inference had been up to me. They had said, we can do anything, even under the eyes of the authorities, even within the heart of their territory. We cannot change the wine into blood, but we can transform it to vinegar. I had not ignored that warning, exactly, but I had hardly heeded it!

El jefe—the Chief, as I had named him—muttered in French to Comstock, the man on the other side of Marie. I could not pick much of it up, but El jefe seemed to be filling the other man in on whatever they had planned for us. This was more than informative. I could tell by the tone of Comstock's brief responses that he was receiving orders.

After a climb and a turn onto a gravel road, the car stopped again. I heard a gate swing open—two doors in sequence on a grinding of hinges. The car continued for a few minutes then stopped again.

"We are here," said the Spaniard. "Well done, Curro."

"Gracias," Curro muttered.

Ah—an employer who likes to keep his people happy! He could kidnap without blinking one of his bulbous eyes, but he had to assuage the earlier reprimand that Comstock had rendered.

Curro muttered something else that was covered up by the opening of his door.

Our blindfolds were removed.

Marie looked slightly annoyed, but unafraid.

"Please pardon the necessity of blindfolding you," said Spaniard, bowing Marie from the car.

We were in a courtyard with a fountain in the center, a Virgin and Child gazing over a plateau on the mountainside from a luminous rainbow of spray.

The house had a ponderous oaken door under a moorish arch of pink bricks. Blue and yellow tiles rose above the arch, and black-barred windows rode down for two stories on either side.

"If you will enter, please," said the man with the Picasso eyes. I decided that he must be Raul Munoz de Armandez, head of POOF. We were not being handled by the underlings! He had come along to make sure that none of the rough stuff one might otherwise expect from the hired thugs did occur, and to keep Curro from losing his job. He was a good driver, but obviously he and Comstock did not hit it off.

We went up three marble steps into a marble antechamber and up some more steps into a vaulted hallway, carpeted and paneled, with a black metal chandelier above.

"Your companion will be shown to her room, Senor Kane. She will join us for dinner. Follow me, please."

I followed him into a paneled library, with an ornate wooden chandelier that played light subtly on the golden leather of bindings on the shelves.

Comstock, the man who had sat next to Marie on the other side followed me, closed the door and stood there at parade rest.

Another man, tall and slender in a light gray suit and pale blue tie, rose.

"Ah, Senor Kane. So sorry to have to interrupt your sightseeing. I am Baptiste Levesque. Please have a chair. Drink?"

His real name? Obviously, these guys had nothing to fear from me.

"Cerveza."

"Of course. Charles!," Levesque said in French, "A beer for Monsieur Kane."

So this was Levesque. Head of GLOP, and another of the three in the picture Marie had taken at the Colon. The third then was the one who looked like an American.

It was too bad that the film had been confiscated—not that having it would do me any good now.

We sat around a giant stone fireplace at one end of the vast library. Occasionally the wind pushed the sour smell of damp ashes across the leather chairs. I downed most of my beer in one swipe—the blindfold had made me thirsty—while the others sipped sherry.

"Is English easier for you?" Levesque asked in English.

"Yes," I said. "I hardly speak Spanish at all."

Levesque laughed a small laugh. I figured the less Spanish I seemed to have, the better off I might be if someone said something significant.

"Why do you think you are here?"

I could have played the sullen, you-tell-me game, but this was a chance for me to direct the discourse for a moment or two.

"I have been, as you no doubt know, conducting some investigations into animal abuse. I am ready to write my report and submit it to the office in D.C."

"The World Watch."

"That's right. I was thinking as we drove up here—Curro is a very good driver, by the way—that you must have some interest in what I am going to say."

"And what are you going to say?"

"Please understand that I have yet to write the report."

I waved my empty glass in the direction of Charles.

"But I have reached my conclusions. There is no doubt that pain is inflicted by the bull upon the horse and certainly agony is inflicted upon the bull. Sometimes it is the banderillas that seem to trouble the bull the most. I am suggesting, however, that bullfighting, that inadequate English word for the corrida, is an element of Spanish culture, like Flamenco—by culture, I mean what man has laid down over nature, in place of nature, sometimes as a reflection of nature, sometimes as a denial of nature. My basic conclusion is that the corrida is a reflection of nature, of death and the man who can kill death but may die as he does so and certainly will die in time. That may seem very existential . . ."

"No, you express it superbly, doesn't he, Raul?"

"I do not love the bulls. I suppose so."

Raul's boredom showed me that the topic was far from the one on the top of his agenda.

"Why should we be interested in your report?" he asked.

Indeed—why?

I gave my best version of a New York City shrug.

"You would have to tell me, and I am pretty sure that you would not. I can tell you this—I have no great commitment to my conclusions. You want me to say that bullfighting is barbaric, atavistic, anachronistic, bloody, and cruel? I will. It is."

Levesque laughed his unamused laugh.

"No. Your report will be fine. I want to know what you heard in Malaga."

I feigned a combination of surprise and bewilderment.

"Malaga?"

"In the bank."

I pretended to search my memory.

"Oh, yes. I did hear two bank managers arguing."

"About what?" Raul asked.

"I don't know. Money, I guess. Look, I can speak enough to get around, but I don't understand much of what is spoken to me. It's too damned fast. So I do not know what they were arguing about."

"But, surely . . ." Raul began.

"Let's leave it at that," Baptiste said. In rapid-fire Spanish, he said, "Enough! If we ask any more questions we begin to provide answers. Bastante!"

Raul shrugged, but he was obviously unhappy. The dynamics here were interesting. These were two of the men Marie had photographed. Both were powerful, yet neither was in charge. It was the third man, then. He was El Jefe. Upper case "J."

I do not like this, I said aloud. I do not like this.

I took another step along the ledge.

I went once with a woman named Sally who taught at the university in New Paltz, New York. She was a rock climber—the typical academic who spent all his or her time doing something other than research and teaching. She could not understand why I wasn't enthralled with clutching a sharp inch of granite with my fingertips while poking my foot through the thinnest of air seeking for a toehold. She spent time on the rockface. I spent time in the bar. Somewhere between cliff and gin, the relationship withered and died. The ledge outside my window was narrow. A treedweller would have been delighted there. After all, King Kong was at ease on top of the Empire State Building.

I do not like this at all, I muttered, sounding like Curro the Barney Oldfield of Andalusia.

I had squeezed past the window of the room to which Charles had escorted me, congratulating myself on staying in such good shape. The window opened in. The bars on the second floor went only halfway up the window, so I was able to crawl up and down and get to the ledge on the side of the building. There was nothing to hold on to from my window to the next. The fall would be only one story—to stone, gravel, or bush—but it would put me out of commission, and I had a fear of the time spent on the way down.

I did not like this.

I slid along until I got to the handhold on the bars outside the next window and held on for a while. Voices floated out past my sweaty right elbow.

They were speaking in Spanish.

"Look, Raul, I do not like this business. We are directly involved in kidnapping, murder."

"Not murder yet, Baptiste."

"There's Baldwin."

"That was suicide."

"Yes. And it was an expensive suicide, even by our standards. One of the underlings went out and bought a hotel."

"It was a small hotel. You must calm down."

"I did not bargain for this kind of criminal activity."

"You mean that you did not want to get this close to it."

"Take it as you will."

Baptiste liked the money. He did not like what went with it—the inconvenient corpse here and there. Still, that was good for Marie and me in the existential present.

"Do you think that Kane knows anything?"

"Nothing important."

"Then we give him a document, apologize for the delay, and send him on his way."

"And the woman?"

"The woman? Of course. She is just along for the ride anyway."

"And that's all?"

"Do you think they'd lodge a complaint? They don't know who we really are—just the official things. They don't know where they are. They want to be free. They will not want anything to do with us again. You don't think we impressed them? Leave the rest to me."

"They saw you, me, and Sebastian together."

"I agree that Sevilla was a mistake, but we had to have those meetings. We had to straighten out the banking situation, encourage that guy from Malaga to retire, set up a new telecommunications network, revise the courier system. Some of that has to be face to face."

"I'm not sure we had to be there."

"Some of that you don't leave to the hired help, Raul. But do you think they'd testify to having seen us? How little you apparently know about how frightened most people are most of the time. And they have reason to be. Sebastian can prove that he was in London on the day they will claim they saw him in Sevilla."

"And so he was. Later. Well, it's Sebastian's decision," Raul said.

"Does he still want to see them?"

"You know he does, Baptiste!"

"Well, he will tomorrow, then."

"And you know what he will do."

"I am afraid I do."

"He will take no chances."

"If you will support me . . ."

"How can I, Baptiste? I think the man knows far more than he lets on."

"I will take them there."

"Do what you want."

I pulled myself carefully around the grille, feeling the metal slide in the sweat of my palms, and continued down the ledge. Fortunately, a drain pipe ran down the corner of the building. I did not put any weight on it, but I did hold on to the pitted surface and breathed for awhile. The long Andalusian afternoon was ruffling the cashmere lawns, and the Virgin wore a halo within the leaping fountain's circle of light. Sebastian? He was the guy who looked like an American. And then I remembered. Sebastian Samuel. I had seen a picture of him coming out of one of those federal country clubs for white collar criminals. What had he been in for? Fraud, insider trading, shady arbitraging. Something like that. He had decided to go not straight, but straight underground. So he was the kingpin? I did not want to meet him.

I was rewarded at last by seeing Marie lying on her back and staring at the ceiling in the next room on the side of the mansion.

I tapped at the window.

She leaped to her feet, came to the window, and mouthed, It's locked!

Yes, they had been careless with me, thinking of the next step on their program, forgetting that I might have one of my own. They were men of wealth, accustomed to believing that the next item on the agenda was theirs to dictate.

Marie motioned me aside. I stepped back to the ledge, holding one bar of the grille.

I heard her go to the door and hit it once with her fist.

The door opened.

"It is very hot in here," she said in Spanish. "Hace mucho calor! Either turn on the air conditioning or let me get a breeze through this window."

The guard muttered something.

"Vali."

I took my hand off the bar, lost my balance, and almost took a dive into the flowers below me.

I heard Marie more clearly through the open window.

"Now, get out of here, Curro! Go! You want me to tell Senor Comstock that you made a move—una mudanza—on me!"

Curro muttered something and left the room. I heard the lock in the door pivot and clunk.

Now, how did I get Marie out of here?

She slid gracefully through the narrow opening.

"Thought you'd come! I didn't want to ruin whatever plan you have."

"So we steal a car. How do we get through the gate?"
"Let's get down first."
"How?"
"That pipe on the corner of the house."
"Okay. Be careful."
"This is nothing. I used to climb. You be careful!"

I did not notice the height as much with another voice encouraging me. I realized suddenly that Marie was buoying me in an emotional sense—and had been for a long time. I almost fell into the flowers.

"Cuidado!" she whispered.

We stood in some bushes at the corner of the building.

"Did you hear what Baptiste said to that other guy on the way up?"

"Some. Not all. What?"

"They are taking us to Villa Franca del Penades tomorrow morning to see someone called Sebastian."

"Villa Franca. Villa Franca. That's on the Costa Durado, below Barcelona."

"So?"

"Too far to drive, even with Curro going like a bat out of hell. That means there's a plane around here somewhere."

I looked out beyond the garages to a fenced hillside. There, pulling toward the east along a final pennant of light was a windsock. And where there was a windsock . . .

Then I heard the dog, barking and coming around the corner.

"Damn!" said Marie.

"I'll deal with the dog. You get behind those garages, go up he hill. Quick!"

I stood on the grass and braced for the dog's leap. A guard dog would come for my throat and I would have to duck and fling the dog over my shoulder. One hundred pounds of flying dog, trained for this moment, mouth pulled back to his incisors? Not likely, but perhaps Marie could get away.

The dog did not jump. Instead, he stopped barking and sniffed at my knees. I had washed this pair of chinos probably a hundred times, but the scent of Casey was in the threads.

"Hola, amigo," I said, ruffling the dog behind the ears with each hand.

I could feel the quivering along the pores that was probably accompanied by that smell that announces I Am Afraid!, but the dog—a mutt with a lot of collie in him—did not respond to my fear.

I had learned that, at times, one must slow down even if the perception is that there's no time left.

"Quieres andar?"

The dog waggled his rear end.

"Vamanos!"

I turned to the line of garages and my friend was at my side. Like Casey, he made friends easily.

Marie was waiting for us in the shadows.

"He's a friend," I said, "but I'll bet they heard him barking!"

The three of us scrambled up the hill, El Perro in the lead, looking back at the slowpoke humans.

I knelt down and took the dog's face between my hands.

"Va a casa, perro."

He looked at me pleadingly, but I was firm.

He padded back down the hill, looking back mournfully over his shoulder all the way.

"How often do you speak Spanish to a dog?" Marie asked.

"The mark of an educated man," I said. "I can speak any man's language—or any dog's. But thank god they did not have a shepherd or a wiemareiner roaming around."

"They wouldn't have. This is neither a fortress nor a hideout."

"They should have had their meetings here," I said.

"Obviously they save this place for smaller conclaves. These guys want to be where the action is."

We looked out from the end of a fence. Darkness had come suddenly, as it will in the mountains, but I saw the plane sitting fifty feet from us in a puddle of moonlight. I looked at the sky. No clouds approaching to give me any hint of cover. A single guard sat on a folding chair at the side of the plane, a rifle between his knees. So they had not discovered that Marie and I were loose on the grounds!

"Stay here!"

I stepped around the fence and strode toward the guard. First step—that he did not shoot me and ask questions after that. Second step—make up a reason for being here. Third step—that my blue eyes did not shine in the moonlight. Fourth step—who knew?

He sprang up and swung the rifle toward me. I heard an ominous click—the safety—as the barrel picked up a glint of moon in its ninety degree traverse.

"Cuidado," I said. "Careful with that. Sr. Comstock sent me out to ask you when you want to be relieved. Your relief is having supper."

"Gracias! My wife is home alone . . ."

I pushed the rifle the way it was going, back toward his chest, and hit him on the side of the jaw with a right. I grabbed the rifle, surprised that it had not gone off, clicked the safety back on, motioned Marie to join me, ripped one sleeve of the guard's shirt, gagged him, rolled him over, bound his arms with the rest of his shirt, and said, "Pull those chocks!"

Just then, a small portable radio crackled to life, beside the folding chair.

I grabbed it and switched it to the reply mode.

"No esta aqui. No hay problemas. Si!" I said, and did not wait for a response.

I grabbed the knife from its sheathe on the guard's belt and hacked away at the ropes holding the plane's wings to hooks on the concrete.

"Okay. Wait here. I'll be right back."

I ran to the shed, wrapped my right hand—which was aching from the shot I had given the guard—in my handkerchief and broke the window. I unlatched it and slid it up.

The moon glinted across the room. I climbed in, pushing the

broken glass aside as I did so. There had to be a flashlight. And there was. Keys hung from eyelets on a board near the door of the shed. Too many damn keys!

I heard the low moan of an alarm, coming from somewhere below me, probably the mansion. Okay—so they had found that we were gone. They'll check the perimeter first.

Keys, keys. I felt like I was swimming underwater. So damned slow. The light splashed back and forth across the panel. Ah!—C 172!

I snapped off the flashlight, unbolted the door of the shed, and ran back to Marie.

Get the right key. Smaller one. I opened the left side, climbed in, opened the right side, then thought to grab the rifle. I got out, climbed back in and handed the rifle to Marie.

"Hold this. And strap in."

"We need it?"

"No. But we don't want them shooting at us with that thing."

I flashed the light around the cockpit.

"Don't mind me," I said. "I am going to talk to myself for a while."

"Go ahead. Can I help?"

"You strapped in? Door locked?"

"Roger that."

"Okay. Fuel Shut Off Valves. On Both. Mixture In. Rich. Carb Head. On. Cold. Throttle. Open one quarter inch. Switch on. Prop Clear. Ignition Switch. Start. Throttle. 1000 RPMs. We've got oil pressure. We'll skip the mag check. Throttle. 1700 RPMs."

I shoved the rudder pedals down and back, pulled the stick back and forth, and waggled it from side to side.

"Flight controls free."

I uncaged the artificial horizon.

"No radio tonight."

I taxied toward the thin ribbon of runway.

"No landing lights. I wonder how long this thing is?"

The lights of a car swung past the shed behind us and glittered in the dishes of the instrument panel, making each one look as if it were holding a spider.

"About 1000 feet," Marie said.

"You have a good eye. 10% of flaps then. Full throttle."

It took a while for inertia—Newton's second law—to release its grip on us. By this time, the car—the same Mercedes that had brought us here from Sevilla—was racing along beside us, to my right, but unless he chose to collide with us, there was nothing he could do. No one was pinging at us with a 45, though, so I held her down, and at 70 knots pulled her up by 5 degrees. Would the runway last? It didn't, but we were in the air. I saw the car behind me swerving expertly to a stop at the end of the runway. Well done, Curro!

"A little less than 1000," I said.

"Enough."

"I'll bet Comstock told Curro to ram us," she said.

"I'm glad they don't get along. Now, sit back and enjoy the flight."

Then I looked at the fuel gage.

Normally, I could count on a tail wind riding down from the hills towards Sevilla's shores as I turned down the long ribbon of river that quivered with moonlight below.

Earlier this afternoon, though, a stubborn camel had twisted his neck in the desert and sent a tremor over the sands that gathered force as it came to Moroccan shores, strengthened as it rode unimpeded to the other side of the old sea and grew to a steady, salty gust that pushed against the fragile windscreen of our motorized kite.

"Close," Marie said, breathing out.

"Still close. Not much gas."

The needle wobbled just at over a quarter full. That would be plenty with a tail wind. Tonight? It would be a near thing. About 90 miles to Sevilla.

"Where to?"

"Back to Sevilla."

"Why?"

"Get you on a plane."

"To where?"

"Anywhere."

"I don't want to split up."

"They will be looking for two of us, Marie."

"What about you?"

"I've got to go back to the hotel."

"They'll be looking for you there."

"I hid some stuff. That position paper I copied. I don't need it, but I can't let them know I've got it."

"You think that would make any difference?"

"They don't know whether we know a damned thing. They might have let us go back there."

"Sure. 'I am going to give you a warning this time.'"

"No. They were being very careful with us. Who knows what might have happened tomorrow. What could we really charge them with?"

"Kidnapping."

"I'll bet they had that covered somehow. Questioning on behalf of the Guardia Civil. MI-6. CIA. They'd know we weren't about to go after them, anyway."

"They probably had orders from the higher ups."

"I think they were the higher ups. At least two of them."

"Don't go back to the hotel!"

"My passport. You have yours?"

"Yes."

"Cash? Credit card?"

"Yes. They didn't pay any attention to me. Frenchman! Spaniard!"

"French Canadian."

"Even worse!"

I flew as low as I dared, to diminish the brunt of the wind, hoping no powerlines drooped across the river. Slow motion again.

If necessary, I'd set down on the train tracks on the south side of the river.

Ah!—we were below Carmona now, gliding down the river basin toward the sea. Sevilla ahead, a splinter of lights curling out along the bend of the river, the bridges black against the gray silk of the Guadalquivir. And there was the rotating beacon of the airport, east of the city, on the Cordoba side. Every little bit helped. The gas gauge bounced against "E." I felt myself straining forward against the straps, like a rider urging his horse over the next jump.

"Sevilla, this is GA 39er9er, VFR from Madrid."

Mix in a little Spanish. Pretend you don't have the Ingles.

"GA 39er9er, Sevilla, go ahead."

"39er9er requests immediate approach to runway 27. No tengo combustible. Demasiado viento."

"39er9er, Sevilla, cleared to land on runway 27. Wind from the south at 12 knots."

"39er9er. Gracias!"

Sput, sputter, ka-pow!

The engine quit as I turned final, but I was high and hot, so we floated neatly over the fence. The runway shouldered around the tiny plane with its lashings of brake marks. I looked down the runway, bringing the long lane of lights back to me, touched down with a gentle kiss, and rolled to a stop on the taxi-strip.

"Yes," Marie said, "that was close."

"Okay," I said, "get to where you can get. Lisbon. Paris. I will catch up with you."

I saw her eyes give me a final concerned glance as she swung from the cabin and took off across the tarmac to the terminal.

She paused, but before she said anything more, I said, "Marie, they won't do anything to us until they find out what we know and whom we've told."

"We haven't told anyone."

"Let's not tell them that. If they find that position paper..."

"You're right! Find me, will you?"

"Right here!"

I had the driver stop just at the entrance to the hotel, a gate, beyond which the driveway curled up to the overhanging entrance and the dozen or so steps to the lobby.

I gave him ten thousand pesetas.

"Bastante?"

"Si, Senor! Gracias!"

I stepped out and looked around. People waited to cross at the light down by the fountain in the Plaza de Jerez. The long avenue behind me—San Fernando—streamed with cars. Under the hotel canopy stood the hotel's beefy doorman and two or three other men. Were they waiting for taxis? No. They were watchful, but in no hurry, smoking and swinging their eyes from side to side—not just to the east from which a taxi would have come. They were waiting for me. Or, maybe not—but it paid to be paranoid. I ducked to my left, down toward the Palos de la Frontera. I walked past the garages to the fence that separated the pool from the street. I had gotten out of shape in only a week, but got over the fence and dropped, breathing hard, to the space behind the small bar that served the pool. I paused for a moment. The rattle of a palm tree startled me. I laughed at myself. I had to go step by step, knowing what some of the steps were, not knowing what others were. I could not afford to let the noises of the night scare me. Now—the side door to the hotel had to be open. It was. But the hardest part still lay ahead. The Alfonso used a heavy brass key holder with keys attached (one for the mini-bar), instead of the new plastic cards to which most hotels had switched. This heavy key was always deposited at the front desk. That's where mine was. I went along the long hall, turned past the gift shop, which was closed, then down the steps into the lobby. I saw Enrique behind the desk to my right. He usually greeted me effusively. I put my fingers to my lips.

"Cien viente, por favor."

I smiled.

He nodded toward the door and slipped the key to me without a word, along with a heavy hotel envelope. I fled back up the steps. I hoped that Enrique would not get into trouble with the boys who expected me to come in at the front door.

My notes were where I had left them, simply mixed in with the stationary on the desk. I folded them up and tucked them in to my jacket pocket.

My passport was tucked into a secret compartment in my attache. But it wasn't.

Where else might I have put it? Bastards!

Okay. I had the notes that would make me a dead man if they'd been found. The lack of a passport was an inconvenience. The air tickets were gone, too. Hell, they'd have at least one seat—mine.

I got a whiff of myself. It was more than a long day, being kidnapped, driven blindfolded to someplace near Cordoba, then stealing an airplane and deadsticking back into Sevilla. It was the sweat of fear. It felt like glue and it stank of something rotten inside, whatever it is that refuses to accept that death, a necessary end, will come when it will come. The fibers of my best Bullough & Jones shirt were now impregnated with the stench, as if it were a dye.

Not yet, I said.

I looked out into the hallway. No one there. Holding the attache—so that I looked like a normal traveler—I went down to the elevator to the pool. As the door slid closed, I saw two men beginning to turn down the long perspective of the hall. The elevator creaked slowly, inch by subtle inch, to ground level.

I got out through the gate below the garbage cans and slid down to Avenida de Portugal. Cab, cab, cab. And there was one.

"Aeropuerto, por favor."

I had thought of going up to Santa Justa, the train station, but decided that I could get something to somewhere further away at the airport. It would all be in the timing. What did they expect me to do? I did not know. I could get to anywhere in Spain as long as a flight would still be scheduled. Could I charter a plane?

They would expect me to try to do something about my passport. They would not expect me just to climb on another plane.

"Barcelona?"

Hurry, hurry. The screen said the aircraft was in final loading process. It was the last plane that would leave Sevilla this night.

The agent kept banging away at keys and staring at the screen in front of her.

"Primero," I said, "Si usted tienes. Passillo, por favor."

First, and an aisle.

It must have helped that I asked for what I wanted. I hoped that she could not smell me from across the counter.

I slipped her a platinum credit card and got a ticket in return.

I got a seat between two others in steerage. A 737 is built for tiny people who do not mind having their space invaded. But I was the offensive person on this trip.

This was a couple with an infant daughter.

"You want to sit together," I said. "I'll move to the aisle."

They were grateful, and so was I.

I had time to go back to the head, wash my face and hands, splash some Iberia cologne over my shirt, and buckle up just as the plane began to taxi.

I would have to get rid of that copy of notes, in case someone met me in Barcelona. Once the seat belt light went out again, I went back to the head, pulled the single sheet back and forth under the tap, then tore the paper into strips and flushed it. Of course, under torture...

I remembered the envelope that Enrique had given me with my key.

"Mesaje de telephono."

What it said was, "Get out quickly. I am in Brussels."

Yes. She would be at the Eurodollar conference. Thanks, Olivia! I'm trying.

I waited, staring at *Diario Andalucia*, while the plane unloaded. I got off with the crew, talking flying with the first officer.

Some official types with a clipboard looked at us, but no one stepped forward to murmur my name with a fatal intonation.

I said adios to Diaz-Alvano, the first officer, and asked what now?

I was in Terminal B. I had pesetas, a credit card. Driver's license? Yes.

The Policia del Aeropuerto were in a corner of Terminal A.

A weary young woman in the blue shirt of a police officer looked up at me from behind her desk.

"Senora, buenas noches. My passport and air ticket were stolen from me in Sevilla."

"Did you report it to the police there?"

"No. I would have missed this flight."

That made no particular sense, of course. It sounded particularly weak in Spanish, but it was a reason. Sometimes harassed travelers do odd things.

I filled out a form. It included the category "Theft by distracting the victim's attention," which I checked.

My driver's license served as my identity card. Without that, I was a man without a country, a person without identity. By now, my friends in Sevilla would know that I was in Barcelona.

The young woman officer took the form and went to some inner office.

I waited, looking at the map of Barcelona.

The young woman returned and handed me a copy of the form. It was stamped with a blue "Oficina de Denuncias, Barcelona" circle, dated and initialed.

"Gracias!"

I would make this a very official document. But now what? If I could hang out for about another six or seven hours, I could talk my way on to a flight to—where? Boston, of course. I had learned that the thing to do is try to trace your original track. My name would be in the computer anyway, but I 'd buy a new ticket. That way, I might just show up as a "no show." I had been planning to stay at the Radisson SAS, where one could sit nursing drinks in the Atrium. I needed an oasis, but I needed an air ticket more than that and it looked like closing time.

My luck had begun to turn. I found a sleepy, olive-skinned Sabena agent taking a last glance at the deserted terminal.

"Brussels. Boston. Manana," I said, just as he was reaching up to pull down the grating on the last open ticket window in Terminal A.

"Passport," he said, resignedly.

"Stolen," I said. "Robo. Here is the police report, my identity card, and my credit card. I'd like (I chose to say, 'I'd like' as opposed to 'I want') first class, aisle please."

Would the document work? Like magic.

"I assume you have no place to stay tonight?"

"I can't leave the airport."

"A moment."

He punched keys and waited while my tickets emerged from the top of the machine, handed them to me, along with my precious document, license, and card, and said, "Wait there, please."

He pulled the grate down for good, then came out, wearing a gray jacket, and said, "Follow me, please."

By now the terminal was empty, the shops were closed and barred, and long shadows flickered under minimum neon and waited for the night staff to sweep and polish them.

We took an elevator up for a very short distance and came out in the lobby of the First Class Lounge.

"Senor, you really can't go anywhere. Questions have been asked. There's a shower behind the reception desk there. Your flight leaves at 1100, Gate 12. Just go up one flight, through security and turn left. You will have no trouble at immigration control, since you are checked through to Boston. But someone is looking for you."

I started to hand him a ten thousand peseta note.

"No. I, too, have been hunted."

To my anglo eyes, he could have been Lebanese, Iranian, or, as my document would have had it in its list of "offenders," either "Arabe" or "Gitana," an Arab or a Gipsy.

"Tienes una chica?"

Do you have a little girl? I had asked.

His dark eyes brightened.

"Como lo sabe?"

"Para ella, entonces."

"Para ella," he said, smiling for the first time and holding out his hand.

No, I thought, my luck isn't changing. It's been with me all the way during this long and interesting day. I had a moment in which to think of Marie during my shower. I set my mental alarm clock for 5:30 and lay down on a couch in the lounge office.

The last images against my half-conscious retinas were of men in suits, smoking and sweeping their eyes back and forth.

"Meet me at Le Meidien, Carrefour de l'Europe."

"I know where it is, but I can't."

"Why not?"

"Two reasons. No passport. And I am trying to get to Boston."

"Without a passport?"

"I'll make it. Meet me at the Sabena Lounge, Terminal A. And, Livy, please bring me a pair of undershorts—cotton flannel, size 36—pants, 36/33, a shirt—17/34—a pair of sox and a sweater—Xlarge. Okay? Oh—and some toothpaste and a toothbrush. I have been travelling light."

"So have I," she said.

She meant since Roger Baldwin had been killed.

I would hope that the beginning of a beard would disguise me—make me look like more of a bum than I looked like already.

It was a dump that lounge, but no one would be there and they'd have plenty of Stella Artois, and I needed a cerveza even this early in the a.m. I would have liked to get in to Brussels, particularly to the Musee des Beaux Artes, where the great Bruegel was. I felt like Icarus. I was flying too close to the sun—the source of power.

And I liked the old cathedral, St. Michel and Ste. Gudule. You wander through the twisted veins of the ancient city and then it leaps in front of you with its huge gothic shoulders. You suddenly know what it's like to believe in God. Today, I could not afford to believe in God.

Hearing Livy's voice had calmed me down. I began to believe I would make it. But what about Marie? I was on my own, but so was she. And—where was she?

"He sent me blindfolded, the son-of-a-bitch."

"No—he couldn't tell you—look what happened—you looked as if you were really looking at the issue of animal rights. If anyone had thought you knew . . ."

"I was looking at the animal issue."

"Exactly. He figured you'd know what to do."

"Well, I don't."

"Didn't, you mean."

"I am not ready to change tenses."

"You will be."

"How do you know?"

"Marie is waiting for you in Boston."

"She is?"

"Yes. Harborside. Take a cab from Terminal E once you clear customs."

I said nothing.

"You think you can get through customs?"

"Once I am in Boston? Of course. But how . . . ?"

"Easy. I was told to tell you."

"What else were you told to tell me?"

"Just that."

She glanced around the room. A couple was checking in at the desk, in French. Smoke drifted in from the smoking room and lurked in thin wisps under the lamps. I cracked open another beer, which spat across that morning's *Le Monde*.

"They do not know how much you know."

She meant to change tense back into the innocent past! I did not see how that could be accomplished. You can't just turn around and take the road not taken.

"So, they are willing to just let things go?"

"I told you. That suicide report on Roger came high. There were inquiries. An inspector of police had to resign when some of the evidence went missing."

"They think I'll just crawl away."

"You'd better. If they had taken you to the other one . . ."

"Samuels."

"I don't know what would have happened. As it is, they've cooled down. You did not go to the authorities in Sevilla . . ."

"As if that would have accomplished a damned thing."

They were right. I told myself that there was nothing I could do. Not even a quixotic gesture was left to me. That they could tell Livy where Marie was told me what they wanted to tell me.

"You report back to them?"

"No. They'll know I saw you."

"Okay. I saw their memo. Roger obviously knew more. Did he tell you?"

"Roger?"

"I just want to know how it works."

"I don't know the details."

"Only a banker would know the details. Okay—I'm still curious."

"And therefore . . ."

"I am not sure about the change of tense."

"What about Marie?"

"You are playing their game, Livy?"

"No! All right."

She paused to sip at her coffee and put the cup down, annoyed. It was empty.

"You go after the issue of animal rights. That calls attention away from what they are doing. The problem was that the puzzle was being constructed to hide what was really happening. They were using part of the money to attack their own organization They were pulling in idealists—Seattle and Washington were funded by their money—to make it look as if workers were being exploited, the environment being ruined—oh, these things are happening—to make it look as if these were the issues, as if the organizations were vulnerable in these areas. Who would look elsewhere?"

"Livy, I know that much."

"So they send one hundred million to combat AIDS. Two million goes to a clinic in Zimbabwe. A million goes to education in the Congo. A million goes to bring doctors to Mozambique. They can point at these things as a response to the protesters, or, as they say, to their awareness of the problem. It takes no protesters to point at the issues. Let's say that only 90 million is left for distribution."

"So they really give the protesters what they want. Great strategy!"

"Of course. They are already funded on both sides. Every cop who says 'It's the American way—to protest peacefully. It's also the American way to let other points of view be heard'—is scripted and on someone's payroll. So are the protesters, though most of them don't know it. People have learned since Vietnam. A few people have learned. They had to discredit the protesters then, because there sure as hell was something to protest. They couldn't fund them. And some people . . ."

"Would not have been bought off."

I was being bought off, of course. Okay. Not everyone was born to take on the naked windmills of the world. Their blades are sharp.

"The scheme was easy. It simply assumed that the rest of the world believed that the big guns were honest men. Money went to an African government. The president's brother is the contractor. He actually does build a toilet, a small dam and generator, a paved road. POOF comes in, takes some pictures of the project and some smiling natives beside it, talks of the improvement of the economy, then closes the books. Most of the money goes back to the government, to a development fund. The ruler and his people take the interest, which makes them fabulously wealthy in their small space. The development fund is used for payoffs, bribes, votes—assuming the country has some semblance of a democracy. Most of the money goes to Swiss banks. Then, once it cannot be traced again, it gets transferred to a bank in Spain. Then—and we are still talking about 90 percent of the money, it gets disbursed to a variety of people, including some functionaries in POOF and GLOP."

Livy's voice suggested that I was not satisfied with what little she had told me.

"You would be surprised how much they had to use in Roger's murder. It's much easier to kill Ron Brown or Vince Foster—there's Pittsburgh money behind that kind of thing. Enough, of course, to raise all those misleading questions about Foster's death in *The Wall Street Journal*—make it look like murder because it was murder."

"Why Foster?"

"A warning. They wanted China. That impeachment bit was a warning too."

"You mean that woman?"

"No. That's the beauty of it. She was very much in love, it seems. The others—starting with that woman in Maryland and right on up, Barr, McCallum, Hyde, the rest. Each had a role to play. They were compartmentalized."

"That's the way they work. They do have their own chart."

"China is a huge payoff," she said. "That bit about Clinton losing his license in Arkansas? A final little sword over his head. The point is not that he wants to practice law. The point is that he won't be able to sit on boards, be a professor here or there."

"He'll have to live off his legal defense fund."

It works partly because no one really gives a damn about the countries involved—that is, unless, of course, we are stopping a communist takeover. The Peace Corps conducts a census for disease control in the Phillipines in the late 60s. So the volunteer are told. They are not told that their census is to control the population as we did not do in Vietnam. We stop the Huk guerillas by knowing who belongs in each village. For the rest of the world—screw them. Henry Wallace was put in charge of one of FDR's wartime committees. His Board of Economic Warfare wanted to make sure that the tin, rubber, copper workers got paid He ran afoul of Jesse Jones, FDR's Secretary of Commerce. The sneering result was the motto "A Quart of milk for every Hottentot." Let them drink chablis.

"It's been a little nervewracking," I said.

"You have a way of putting things mildly."

"Yes. What now?"

"Oh—here's a note I was told to deliver to you."

I looked at the handwriting on the envelope. "Larry Kane." It was not Marie's writing. I put it in my right pants pocket.

"Next for me? I only have a notion, but Roger and I bought a place on Siesta Key.

It's one of the last ones left down a dirt road, through a jungle, then an inlet with a wharf and a neat, clapboard cottage. I am going to vegetate for a little while."

"Far from the hum of all those malls on the Tamiami Trail."

"Too close. But there's a grocery store around the corner. Tennis courts. I know some people. The beach. It will take time."

"Yes."

"I would admit that to no one but you."

I don't think either of us wanted to get into a personal discussion. I know that I didn't.

"Thanks for the duds. I am going to change in the men's room and get down to the gate. I still have another control point to talk my way through."

"Keep in touch, Roger."

I nodded. I would see her sooner than I would have believed.

I left the fear-stained clothes in the men's room, remembering to shift the note Livy had given me to pocket of the Polo chinos she had selected for me. I was a new person, dressed ready to begin the morning right and face the undocumented journey.

It wasn't until I was enscounced in a great lounge chair in Sebena First that I felt the note scratching against my right leg.

It was a woman's handwriting—neat, precise, youthful.

"Your guardian angel has no more miracles left. D."

Okay—so I have run out of miracles. I did not know I had any in the bank, so it can't be counted as a loss. D? Who the hell was D? In novels, Henry James or Edith Warton bring people back after years in some remote corner of their imagination, but in life, people go off and do not return. My daughter, for example. Life does not have the symmetry of fiction, which is why a lot of people prefer fiction. But D? I pushed one of several buttons on the arm of my seat and pushed back. I was suddenly exhausted. I would drowse the way to Boston as the great screen in front of me showed our Airbus sliding from one of the round earth's imagined corners to another.

"More wine, Mr. Kane?"

Who knows? I might even sleep.

"Uno mas, por favor."

Yes. It had been ten years ago. I had just been divorced. I was pretending to enjoy the new life at hand in which I could make any decision I wanted to make without negotiation—I mean a fight. I could have been trying to convince her to leave a burning house. She would have fought me. Well, that was over. The city was refusing to yield to spring, so I did the logical thing. I pointed my new car north.

An old record spun by in the background. It was the blue of evening, when crickets call and stars are falling. So said the voice of early Frank Sinatra, when it had a sweetness and vulnerability, just after Harry James, just after the Paramount in New York, and long before he began to do it his way. It was a lost time. The Appalachian accent of Keeley Smith said "As You Desire Me." Fire scissored into the rings of the damp log I had just placed on the embers. They dropped, blue-red-yellow-green, into an oblivion of ash. Above, the old sailing ship in the painting seemed to plunge though a pulse-beat of sea that rose and fell and moved the clipper's figure head up and down in the wash of dark and a sudden gold that burned the undersides of the brushstrokes. A couple of candles moved two and fro on the table. Day was done. Keeley was touching on the possibility. *I miss you most of all when day is done.*

"Days are getting longer."

"Right side of the power curve," I said.

"We get an afternoon again."

I went around the corner to the fridge and returned with two beers in hand. I sat on the couch next to her.

"Why not? Just for a while."

"Larry, I don't have to say why. That opens up a debate. Negotiations. Don't try to manipulate me. No."

I took a long pull from my Molson. She was wearing a flannel nightgown, shapeless except where she shaped it. I rubbed my hand over that crunchy cotton and decided not to pout.

"Tell me what you're working on," she said. That is, if it won't ruin the creative drive."

"Creative drive? It's a case of getting up in the morning and going to work. It's a version of 'The Fall of the House of Usher.' Ever read it?"

"Sure. I read all of Poe by the time I was twelve."

"I read 'Usher' one night when I was alone in our big, drafty house in New Jersey. Scared the Easter Bunny out of me. That's where the creativity comes in—calling back that original response in the crafting of the play. Anyway, narrator . . ."

"Name?"

"Remember in the story, he has none. We—you, the reader—become the focal point of the story. 'Madman! We have put her living in the tomb!' I remember the creshendo of fear, as if I were sitting at the center of the cymbal section. It was the feeling, not the sound. Then, the cellar door crashed down in the wind and I fled to the safety of bed, leaving the big light in the living room burning. Cost a lot to burn that light in those days. So I was told the next morning. I am working on a complete character for

Madeline, not just a pale presence glimpsed down the hallway. Of course the narrator falls in love with her, but that won't work. He may see her sneak to Roderick's room one night for a forbidden tryst. The house is surrounded by a vast zone of swamp and broken trees. She can't leave it, of course. She's the resident deity."

"Like what's her name."

"Who?"

"In the story."

"Eleanor."

"Yes, in the Shirley Jackson story."

It may have been the fires of first meeting, but we did seem to ride the same intellectual rhythms. That was something else that would probably have faded and become a point of contention later on, but no later on would interfere with the quick completing of each others' phrases .

I had not yet dropped into the paralysis of despair or the dry routine that alone insists that the legs get swung to the chilly floor each a.m., and I had yet to move to Maine. Nor had Katherine had that fight with her mother and suddenly arrived on my doorstep to spend the dark and savage teen years with me. That had been five years before I had acquired the wonderful Casey. The place on Cape Cod would be empty until renters moved in for Memorial Day and a key hung on a nail on one of the posts in the garage. I did need to get out of the canyons, raw with penetrating damp and away from the gaunt buildings, etched soullessly against a sky gray by day and steel by night in the never-ceasing light that made the stars a mythology of ancient man.

I aimed the Volvo toward Boston. Rain moved back and forth in front of me like the bows of a ghostly violin section, but Bix and Bunny, Yank and Muggsy, Red Nichols and Charley Teagarden played from the tape. I had had only a radio before and the stations I needed tended to drift away among the toll booths and snorting semis behind me. I would listen involuntarily to stories of tenement fires, municipal corruptions, skidrow murders, drug convictions and mayoral posturing. It was easier driving as Charlie Turner flew above the normal range of "Time After Time." I tried to avoid driving as the Romans do. If a Massachusetts driver ever hurt his left index finger he or she would be unable to drive.

I slid down toward Route Six and traffic thinned. No one wanted Cape Cod on a rainy Tuesday. The state cops would not have one of their massive speed traps concealed behind the dunes and scrub pines just as the thirsty drivers began to savor g and ts on the patio overlooking the beach. I could cruise at 70 with my new cruise control and listen to Helen Ward come in over Benny's clarinet on "I'll Never Say Never Again," wishing I had said it long ago and wondering when I'd get a chance to say "again" again.

The bridge rose like a tracing in charcoal beyond the empty traffic circle. No barges or boats made wakes on either side of the thin span. I began to believe that I was in the middle of an atomic attack. Nothing moved except the arms of Gene Krupa, banging out a tomtom solo on "Sing Sing Sing." The world would vaporize and exit to the sycopating trumpet of Harry James.

The sky began to clear to a blank white above the pine and maple and by the time I passed the I.L.S. stanchions outside of Hyannis, I could roll the window down with my automatic switch. The filthy air that clumped over the mainland rarified to a whispy thinness, then to a milky diffuseness, with blue drifting to the surface. Suddenly, it was May. Ziggy Elman ripped into the rollercoaster of "The Angels Sing."

I turned on to 6A and stopped in Brewster for a case of Molson Golden.

I put a dozen bottles in the fridge, slung my Puma bag on top of the couch that turned into a bed, and changed into a pair of tennis shorts, an old sweatshirt and my brickdust impregnated Jack Purcells. I headed across the Cape on Route 28 to Chatham, passed the Chatham Bars Inn, which had not opened its doors or its rows of hyacinths yet, went past the corner that led to many shoppes, and turned down Water Street. I parked in the last driveway on the left and walked down a path that was rotting away the edges of the dune. I dragged a tiny skiff by the painter from a shed and down across the shingle.

The water wrapped my sneakers in sudden ice. I pushed off and jumped in, pulling a muscle in my back. I unshipped the oars and pulled across the bay. I was sweating by the time I began slipping through the grasses on the other side. My back ached, but the arms and legs felt good, responding to the stretch and pull, the flex and release of untended muscles. The water roiled away in spinning green 78s against the small gray waves of the bay. The scene of years before rose from the wake, along with the sadness that went into seeing those years ride away within their green circles. The sun began to burn the white knob on what had been the bridge of my nose, under the sweat that dribbled from my forehead. I had forgotten that tennis and squash had developed my right arm far out of proportion to my puny left, so I had tracked far to the left of my intended spot of disembarkation.

But so what? When I had been a kid, walking in the woods or jumping into the water, I had had no concept of enjoying that freedom. To know I had been free would have been to lose the quality in the concept. But now I knew that people could rise high and never be free. They could only envy adolescence—its arrogance, its insensitivity, its sexual abundance, its blessed righteousness, its narcotic sense of certainty, its vicarious mimicry of achievement, where grace is in the objects, but where no claims for transubstantiation are made for them. You must, therefore, get more of them.

I dragged the skiff up above the woven straw that marked the last high tide and walked up the spine of the outer beach through the bending grasses. The wind was steady from the east, sending five and six foot waves onshore, spilling in giant, golden fleecings over the bar, a hundred shallow yards from where I stood. Out there, the wind-roughened water was slatey-gray. Deeper. I watched for a while, picking up the wave I would ride and letting it bring me in, visualizing the experience as present-day coaches say to do. The waves looked like small mountains on the move, but they were actually cylinders formed as the water spilled over the sandbar and curled back to churn in and collapse at me feet. They bowed, as if saying, at your service. I took off my "Amherst Lacrosse" sweatshirt, slid out of my Jack Purcells, tossed them on top of the shirt, and stepped into the foam.

"Cold!" I said aloud.

The salty scent of death rode back into the ooze of sand. In August, this wasteland would stink of suntan oil and last-night's lovemaking, a haze of suntan and moonburn.

The water numbed my ankles.

The worst part is to get waist deep. No. Third worst. The worst is to splash that frozen liquid over chest and shoulders. The second worst is the final plunge under the first breaking wave. The next breath seems a long way away. Cold and a seething sand-filled roar pressed on my brain as I treaded water out beyond the spot where the smaller waves were slipping past the bar. My body was numbing, every sinew, every marrow-lined bone filling with hexagons of ice. My teeth ached. My motions were becoming spasmodic. I let several waves lift me and watched them race in green-veined fistfuls toward the shore. One gray wall nodded at me. I nodded back.

I swam toward the wave, almost up to it, then wheeled with my right shoulder. I swam hard for the shore, even as I was raised back into the shoulders of the wave. For a moment, I was poised far above the chop and was about to roll back into the wave lest I be slapped down on that rocky surface below, like a fish being smitten to death against the splinters of a wharf. The wave broke, sliding my chest down its inner curve, suddenly alive with rainbows. I pulled my shoulders forward, flattened them, put my head down into the friendly waters, and was of the wave. I popped my head up a couple of times to sip a quick breath and found myself at last on my knees, digging holes in the sand as the last of the wave dropped away to a memory just past, like a lover leaving. I crawled away from the sea, numb except for the pull of waters I still felt in the leaden muscles. I let the lengthening angles of afernoon and the sand-strewing lower wind dry me.

I stood, muscles still taut, stomach ridged with a freeze-dried sinew that had emerged from a lagered paunch. I pulled on my sweatshirt, scrunched into my sneakers and turned to look at the sea. Clouds bunched down from the northwest, flexing muscles against the falling afternoon. The waves marched. Okay, Mr. Death. There was your chance. For today. I wondered whether my lips were blue.

The wind caught on an edge of evening. I could barely pull the skiff back into the shed. Had I drowned, the skiff would have drifted away, down the tide and out to sea at the far end of the bay. Someone would have found my car, maybe even my shirt and sneakers.

"Fool went swimming in April. Water temperature 58 degrees."

"Suicide."

"Didn't leave a note."

"Some writer! Just another lousy play on the way. Good riddance!"

My friends would find the skiff or, more likely, replace it. They would not even report it stolen. It was something, which, like a vapor or a drop of rain, once lost, would stay that way.

That night, after a long shower, many beers, a tv-dinner that would have tasted better had I cooked the succulent-picture on the box it came in, and half a murder mystery, I pulled out the sofa bed and closed my eyes. Waves rose in front of them. A roar churned in my ears. My body warmed under a woolen blanket. I heard the tide rise in the bay outside my window and felt marrow and sinew let their ice out. Whatever I dreamed, rank after rank of waves rode under the images. The waves were all I remembered in the morning.

I had a couple of cups of coffee, then left "Kasa Kane," as mother had named it, and drove up the windswept and deserted 6A to the Orleans Mall. There, I bought a *Times*, eggs and bacon, burger and rolls and a three pack of Lacoste sox at the Puritan Clothing Store. The crocodile did not attract me, but the ease of getting sox on in the morning did. That is a feature that people who live alone with their bad backs must consider. I drove back to Brewster, under maples flipping white sides up as storm approached. I turned down to the bay, where white waves drove at the beach and sky hurtled over the target ship rusting in Wellfleet Harbor. I pulled up beside the cottage and pushed the door open against the wind. The rain now rode parallel to the bay. The door to the shower stall had come loose and banged back and forth. I pushed it closed, put the rope back over the post and wedged a shingle in to the gap. I'd fix the damned thing tomorrow. The renters would come and expect perfection for their thousand a week. I walked around the front, holding my hand against the salty bite of the rain. The unprotected side of the seawall was eroding. The wall would become a hollow shell and the cottage would tumble in behind it. If I worked on that side, though, I would weaken the root structure of sea grass and beach plum and hasten the seepage of erosion. Already, I had worn an unintended path over the roots that held the dune together. Seawalls were prohibited now, because of the wave effect that drags the sand away from the base of the wall. It was too late now to persuade the guy next door to put a wall in. His cottage looked as if it were about to fall face forward into Cape Cod Bay.

I checked the steps. They were as secure as they had been in September and sat solidly on the wall, below the long walkway that led down from the flagstone patio. The bottom section sat in the grasses above the wall, ready to be put in place. Tomorrow.

The wind seethed and tossed more water into my face, half-rain, half bay. Time to prepare some superb burgers, have the first of several beers, then jot some ideas for "Usher." The sounds of storm would help.

I glanced down the beach.

Damn!

A set of steps lay along the edge of the high tide mark on top of driftwood, straw, and loose seaweed. I leaned into the wind and looked next door. Yes, the steps had been ripped away by a recent storm. I went down our steps, then edged out over the slick rocks and jumped to the heavy sand, which hit back against my kneecaps. The steps were now awash. Another half-hour and they would be on their way to sea, past the last curling fingertips of Race Point, beyond the invisible lighthouse which marked the beginning of the North Atlantic.

Damn! They were heavy, each vein thick with water. I picked up one side, dragged it, picked up the other, dragged it, and was making progress to which the base of my spine talked back. Would I go into spasms here on this salt-tormented strand?

A voice came to me on the wind.

"Need some help?"

She wore a yellow slicker that matched the whispers of hair pasted to her forehead. Her green eyes sent back the silvery flash of the rain, as if the storm were there, excited, behind her gaze.

"Almost finished. Let's drag it up to the edge of the bank."

She looked beyond me, out to the bay.

"It will still wash away."

"Trust me."

We left the steps there and clambered up the bank. The wind was heavier on top and the rain bit like pellets.

"Wait for me in my car. You've earned lunch and a beer!"

I pointed past the cottage to my gleaming blue Volvo.

I had to pull the pocket of my soaked jeans inside out to get the key to the tiny door of the cinderblock basement under the cottage. I removed a coil of rope from a cobwebbed nail, snapped the lock again, and bent my way down the beach. I drove our neighbor's dune forward in great gobbets in front of each step. I tied one end of the rope to the steps with a harness hitch and the other end to the main posts from which the steps had parted. The rain sounded like bullets against my slicker.

I sat in the car, catching my breath and blowing at the combination of rain and sweat that dribbled down my uneven nose. My sneakers were filled with drying sand.

"Now someone will come along and steal both steps and rope," I said, laughing.

"They aren't even yours?"

"Negative. Or maybe the steps will pull the rest of the system with them out to sea."

"Are you always this pessimistic?"

"Only about things that don't count. How did you happen to come along?"

I turned to look at her. Early twenties, with that clarity of skin and eyes that balanced on the far edge of adolescence. I caught my breath and let it out as if I were still recovering from my recent exploits.

"I love storms. Besides, the wind was at my back."

"Downhills have uphills."

"I have a ride now, don't I?"

"Yes. I am not sure who lucked out, though."

"My name is Dorothy."

"I won't say it. You are the heroine of a Charlotte Bronte novel. And you are getting hungry, very hungry."

"I was when I happened upon your imitation of Winslow Homer."

She had driven to the Cape from Western Massachusetts. Yes, from Williams. To be by herself, she told me, in a throaty voice that did not match the limber quality of the rest of her. You would not have been able to match voice and face, but the two synchronized when you heard her smile. She was staying at LaSallette, once a nunnery, not a sybaritic condominium.

"You can't be alone at college. You are supposed to be in the process of socialization."

"It didn't take with me," I said.

We found a restaurant wedged into the intersection of 6A and 28 in Orleans.

We were the only ones there. I felt that rare resonance surrounding the table. We were in the zone. I touched the top of her hand.

"Where are you going to be?" she asked.

"You were just there."

"Drop me at my car at the end of Ellis Landing. I was on my way back to school"

"Now?"

"I will be going back a little later."

"You sail?" she asked.

"Bad back," I said. "And knees."

She brushed a veil of disappointment from her eyes.

"Just as well," she said.

Three days later, on our last evening, as moonlight dusted the pine trees in the back of the cottage, I was trying to negotiate a future. Running on the beach, having her hipcheck me into pools waiting for the tide's return, wandering around a boarded up and wind-rattled Provincetown, talking ceaselessly when we weren't making love—I wanted more. I wanted to find out what the source of the light in her eyes might be. Three days was not enough.

"You are more of an existentialist than I am," I said.

"No. I know what I want. I have become accustomed to what I have. I cannot see eating tuna fish from an ironing board while brats bawl in the near distance."

"That's your Williams education talking."

"Yeah. It has nothing to do with existentialism. I am a practical little wasp who can turn into a bitch very easily. Don't you see beyond the infatuation?"

"No. That's no fun."

"It was wonderful, though."

"Is."

"Is."

Ashes came alive as they dropped from the grate in prismatic explosions. She reached back and pulled her flannel gown up and over her head with a single motion. She slid in front of me, the young body a breathing sculpture, her green eyes filled with flame.

"That's nice, kiddies," she said. "Don't quarrel."

"I know I'm not in Kansas."

"Me Dorothy."

The next day, cold and smelly like a doused fire, I listened to Dinah Washington sing "Willow, Weep for Me." I fixed the door on the shower, put the bottom section of steps onto their hinges, then drove southward, through desolations of April. Dorothy! You never get a view of the city from here. You are in it. Too damned soon!

She had told me she did not believe in witches, wicked or otherwise. She had said that guardian angels, though, were always hovering near. Somehow—it must have been after Marie and I had flown to Sevilla on fumes—she had learned that I was on the wrong side of the Monopoly board from—it had to be Samuels—and she had persuaded him to let me go. Well, she hadn't lingered with a broken down playwright. Was she trying to tell me something? Yes—that she remembered, and that she had no regrets about that few days ten years ago, and none about not making it last any longer.

IV.

"Yes, but I'm starving. Aren't you?"
"They fed us on the plane. I am grungy."
"Can you be grungy and hungry?"
"If you say so."
"Nobody else."
"That's right."
"So—meet me at the Rialto."
"Venice?"
"Charles Hotel. Cambridge."

Our reunion was subdued, but it was good that it was in casual Cambridge, where I fitted right in, looking like a rumpled graduate student who had suddenly been given a credit card.

The restaurant resembled a living room, with velour sofas and chairs, and standing lamps. Marie's eyes returned the light in that shadowy space as if they were their own source of light.

"No. They told me to wait for a day or two. You'd be along."
"How did they know?"
"Of course they knew. I got enough pictures of old ships to start a line of postcards."
"No force?"
"No. I was free to take the room or not. They said they would get word to you."
"They did."
"How?"
"Livy Baldwin."
"Oh, yes. Your ex."

"Don't knock it. She brought me the very clothes I am wearing. My others got a bit messed up. I left a seventy five dollar shirt in a men's room in the Brussels airport. You had no trouble?"

"It went beautifully. Last flight to Madrid. I had time to have the Inglaterra send my bags to Iberia. London. Boston. The message came to me at Gatwick, South Terminal, just before my plane took off."

"They knew before I did."

"Maybe. Maybe they just figured out what you would do."

"Yeah, what anyone would do—trace the original route."

"No—what you would do. Most people would truck themselves into the American consulate. I'm not knocking it, by the way. You make me out to be a possessive bitch. You are free, after all."

So are you, I thought. That's the problem. The old double standard has not gone away. But I did not want to fight with Marie. She was too beautiful and here we were reunited after a couple of days that could have been dangerous. They seemed to be, in retrospect, and yet, since they had not proved so, they seemed to be some sort of diversion that needed to be figured out. Things that had happened before we had been kidnapped seemed closer in time. When I looked back on the past couple of days, they seemed to be inevitable. They hadn't been. If they had flown us north the next day . . . Well, they hadn't.

"No. I am just a little tired."

"All those beautiful women."

"Only two this time. I can still feel the sand in my shoes. And, yes, tengo hambre."

"You have been dreaming again, my sweet. I recommend the marinated chicken. It is cooked under a brick and served on wild mushrooms."

"Mushrooms actually caught in the forest primeval? I sometimes feel as if I have been cooked under a brick."

She laughed.

"We will get you some clothes, dear heart, and a long shower. I will scrub your back. Not with a brick!"

The *soupe de poisson*, seasoned with basil and garlic, raised ghosts between us, and we paused on that note of agreement.

"And you are going to do nothing," she said, glancing to the left and right along the carved oak frame of her chair.

I also looked around the room. I took a sip of the 1989 white wine Marie had ordered for us. I felt my pores—in need of soap and hot water, but no longer cooling and heating with the sensations of pursuit.

"I have thought about it. That does look good," I said, as the chicken arrived, sans brick, but vivid—for chicken—under its red pepper marinade.

"You can ask to lick the brick," Marie said.

"Later. The problem is, my love, that no one in the world is honest enough and powerful enough to take on these bastards. This is not a decision that I am making. Anyone honest enough would be bought out in a minute—or killed, though they have learned to avoid killing. It's like the Donne poem. 'Though she last 'till you write your letter . . .'"

"In this case, 'he.' It's the men who are the whores.'Tell me where all past years are.'"

"That's one question. These bastards could tell us who cleft the devil's foot. They were there at a planning session."

We grew quiet over our wild mushrooms and second bottle of Vina Mayor Ribera.

"You know . . ." she said.

"You're right," I said.

"I don't want you taking off again so soon!"

"Marie, my one true love, it can't be done by phone."

"I guess not. I know you're taking off when I hear you call me your one true love."

"And coming back," I said.

"Si, esta in Florida."

"Florida. Estados Unidos?"

"Yes, Senor Kane. He told me to give you this number when you called."

I called again.

"Meet me at Carrabba's. The one on Stickney Point. Tomorrow. Seven. I'll have a corner table. It's noisy enough so we will not be overheard. But be careful, Lorenzo."

I saw the anxiety in Marie's eyes before I turned from her at Gate 6, Delta to Atlanta.

"Be careful."

"I am the soul of caution," I said.

My seat number was 2B.

Or not to be, I said to myself.

My bag did not arrive with me, but would be on the next flight from Atlanta I was told, so I took my rental car across the highway and walked into the rose gardens beside the Ringling Museum and sat on a bench in the sun. I realized that I had not merely sat on a bench at noon in a long time. Clouds, like chubby angels at the limit of cartography, blow with fattest cheeks against a sun, far from frozen creeks and icy bootprints and the white ground, moonlit and long in shadows of northern stars. A rose is taboo there, but here a secret birth rises from the laughter lines of earth, grand finale of a new day, verbose with blossoms. For a moment, all the warm can play upon my pores, and eyes again can rise above the huddle of the storm and view the polar star through daylight's curtain, north of here, beyond the cumuloform of the Gulf, where pregnant cherubs spill with rain. I think back to the contrast between damp cold Montreal and the sudden orange trees of Sevilla. I breathe deeply. That all seems in the distant past, as intense memories seem to be—no matter how recent. They become tiny, like things seen by the childish eyes focussing themselves to whatever big, dark reality may turn out to be.

Lo and behold—my bag is riding the carousel awaiting my liberating grip! I realize that I still have memories of travelling sans luggage from Sevilla to Boston with stops in between for a deep breath or two, and a few cervezas.

"I knew you'd be back in contact," Don Alvaro said.

I looked down at my sirloin marsala to decide how to attack it. I would cut on the bias, slicing thin medallions, rare surrounded by a uniform crispy edge. I rinsed my watering mouth with a sip of Napa Merlot.

He was right. The noise bounced against our corner booth and stayed there, a kind of shield.

"Como?"

We were speaking in Spanish. It felt good to relax into the crunch of "crs," the lilt of the drawn out consonant, and the breathing vowels.

"That is why I left my number with my housekeeper. I am here to see family and to work out some problems in the export sector of my business. But you asked how. One learns to read the bulls. It is almost automatic when one looks at a human face. Bulls are mucho mas complicado."

I laughed.

"I cannot read faces, Don Alvaro. Or perhaps it is that in this country, one reads the same thing."

"Oh, yes," he said, "the signal is usually the same. It is the 'how' and not the 'why' that one must learn to read."

I told him what more I had learned.

"Yes, I could feel your hesitation when you visited my ranch. That's all right, Lorenzo. This is dangerous. It will not be dangerous when I get it into the Spanish courts."

"You can do that?"

"At least part of the criminality resides in Spain. That is a difficult issue in these days of open, electronic borders. Spain is very anxious to gain respect on the continent. Yes. We can get that little weasel from Malaga. He knows enough to open the thing up. I know some good lawyers, Lorenzo, and most judges would not dare to contradict the evidence we will bring. It was Spanish law that was broken, basically, and the suit will rest on the narrow grounds of financial malfeasance. But the process will have the backing of the European Union so it will run its proper course."

That phone call to the King might finally be made.

"What insures that the process will run smoothly is that the big boys will know that they will get off. What the court will do is put an end to their practices. They will deny any involvement, and they have covered themselves. They have been careful never to have been seen together, even when they were at the same conference or meeting. They made sure they were never in the same public room."

"And the court cannot deconstruct that fact?"

He laughed and took a sip of his Ybor City dark beer.

"That itself would be conclusive to some people wouldn't it? but it can never be introduced to any court of law. The point is that they won't dare do this kind of thing again. Oh, for a long while, at least. They will be under scrutiny. That will be a good. Oh—they may even pay some fines for violation of banking practices. But the flow of aid to the millions who need it should go smoothly."

And the smooth and superbly tailored men will go free to their billions.

"Nothing else can be done," I said. It was not a question.

"Justice is a limited thing in practice. But it defends you and me as well. The defense will insist that they are not connected. Until you make that connection, you cannot make a case."

"The prosecution will say that the case makes itself."

"The defense will say that paper will prove anything. These transactions are complicated. They can prove that the money went where it was meant to go, and that, if crimes were committed . . ."

"Even if the money came back."

"Yes—hidden in this or that fund. Inference is overpowering, I agree, but inference, in a Spanish court at least, will not weigh in the scale."

My room looked out over the length of an inlet. At one time, I would have had a view of sunset over the Gulf, but now two huge condos stood out there along the beach, waiting for one of John D. McDonald's hurricanes. Still, I got some wedges of western sky, and a final boat came in through the glittering ripples of sunlight and tied up, its windows on fire. Time for me to climb into my rental, go down 41 for a couple of blocks, cross the Ringling Causeway toward St. Armand's and then cut across 780 to Longboat.

"I am really sorry that Tim can't be here."

She had explained to me on the phone that her new friend, Tim something-or-other, would be unable to join us. Out of town on business. She had really hoped that I could meet him.

"Sorry."

"So am I."

Tim was a fiction, of course, a character invented to let me know that Olivia was doing very well, thank you, back on her feet, on her way again, just fine, as desperate people like to say, as my ex-wife used to say. Just fine. And, maybe Olivia was saying that she was not going to sleep with me tonight. It might be simply a polite way of putting that issue out of the way for both of us. There was still a resonance. I could see it trembling on the surface of our glasses of Marcelina Cabernet Sauvignon.

"More wine?"

"I'll finish this and have a brandy."

I would give her Tim. He was a useful construct. It put limits around our evening that were necessary for both of us.

I resisted the impulse to hold my glass up and say, Here's to Tim.

"He's the main reason I wanted you to come down, really."

Yes, yes, I said to myself, and I saw in her glance at me that she knew I didn't believe her.

"No, the real reason—and this can only be conveyed face to face—is to say that the big boys do not know where the accusations and evidence came from. They think it was from a Spanish source, perhaps the former manager of a bank in Malaga."

I remembered him. A man of conscience in a tank of sharks.

"They retired him. Made him an errand boy."

"Yes. They aren't sure, and, since it's known that they suspect him, they don't want to make a move against him. It would only substantiate the case against them. As it is, they'll get off".

"That's what Don Alvaro says. Dammit!"

"All they have to do is keep denying they know each other, have ever seen each other. The paper trail is inconclusive, and a lot of money has gone into a lot of pockets."

"Damn!"

"The point is, Larry, that with the attention that has been directed to their operation, they won't dare try this kind of thing again. Your sense of justice will just have to remain unfulfilled. Why do you men have to have everything complete?"

"Sense of symmetry. But I suppose I should be happy to be alive, to have had a juicy prime rib with horseradish and Kona fried onions, and a good bottle of wine, and to be across the table from a smoky woman like you."

"Two good bottles of wine. Count your blessings."

"The second bottle made me lose count."

A voice came down from behind her.

"Got your 'just in case' message. Can I join you for a coffee?"

It was Tim. Tall, sandy-haired. A sailor probably. Maybe a college professor.

His out of town business had obviously been negotiable.

Olivia took in a great gulp of gratefulness.

I stood and shook hands with him.

"I've heard a lot about you," I said. "We are going to have a brandy."

"That sounds about right. Livy has given me a brief outline of some of the adventures you two have had recently. I don't want to know any more."

"No, you don't," Olivia said, laughing and taking his hand. "Oh, I'm so glad you're here!"

"Meet me at Jackson's. South Harbour Island Boulevard. 1230."

"Who the hell is this?"

"A car will pick you up at the Hyatt at 11:45. Just be there, Kane."

I was.

"He'll recognize you," said the man who had ridden silently up Route 75 with me, as we walked out from under the shadows of the parking garage, past a noisy noontime bar. He pointed to a terrace overlooking the Hillsborough River.

A man raised a suited sleeve as I came down the steps.

Ah!—it was the third man in Marie's missing photograph.

"You must be 'See No,'" I said as I got to the table.

He gave me his 'I do not suffer fools gladly' look and indicated a chair.

"I'm Samuels."

Sebastian Samuels—the reclusive arbitrager and deal-maker, known as the Howard Hughes of Wall Street. He had grey eyes, a tanned face, a taut gut, and the habit of twisting his right fist in a clockwise motion in the palm of his left hand. He looked like someone who did not make his own reservations. At the same time, though, I figured we would be an even match, unless, as was probable, he had mastered some exotic form of self-defense. Boxers are helpless against people like that. You throw out a left jab and you find yourself flat on your back.

"Drink?"

"Draft."

"I took the liberty of ordering sandwiches, Mr. Kane. You have no special dietary restrictions."

It was a statement. They had probably been sitting at the next table at many restaurants since my trip to Montreal.

"Too kind," I said.

"You are going to do two things, Mr. Kane."

"I hope more than two."

"For me, I mean. You are going to sign this affidavit . . ."

He took a paper from a blue plastic folder and held it up.

"And you will submit your report."

The report, of course, would be a further sign-off from me, making it all look so routine and legitimate.

"The affidavit says that I have never seen you with two specific other gentlemen."

"Words to that effect."

It was possible that once I signed the paper, I disappeared. His mention of the report sketched in a future that he did not intend for me. It was like the Nazis telling the Jews to remember where they had left their clothes before they took their showers.

Our sandwiches—roast beef on rye with horseradish sauce and lettuce—arrived, along with my beer.

"Another beer," I said.

"And then, of course, you get paid. Possibly a bonus, if they like your report as much as I think they are likely to."

"Your money is sticky with Baldwin's blood, and that of a lot of people who are starving in Africa even as we munch."

"Don't get moralistic on me, Kane."

"Anything that verges on the truth becomes moralistic in your world, doesn't it, Samuels."

The pupils in those gray eyes grew small, in spite of the sunlight splashing at us from the river and from the windows of the Westin Conference Center across from where we sat.

"I will not bandy words or philosophical nuance with you, Kane. Sign the paper, please."

I made no move to take it from between his thumb and forefinger.

He slipped it into the blue folder again and produced a cell phone.

He punched some numbers. I counted. It was a local call. He said something into the phone, and handed it to me.

"Larry?"

It was Livy.

I missed a beat.

"Yes. You okay?"

"I am here of my own free will."

"Of course. I'll come and get you."

Samuels reached for the phone. I held on to it. I had some notion—what gave it to me, the lift of his eyebrow, my own tiredness that induced paranoia, the intuition at which I usually sneered until I was living the moment I had predicted—who knows? He would have said something to whomever—Comstock—and it might not be good. I tossed the phone into the Hillsborough River. Comstock—whoever—was communicating for a moment or two with bubbles dropping into the eternal muck of the river bottom. A couple of people had seen the flight of cell phone 101 and feminine laughter rose and died above a nearby table.

Samuels looked at me, naked rage vivid for an instant in his eyes.

I had destroyed *property*, more important by far than human life.

"You fool!" he hissed. "We are being observed. You are fortunate that a very fast moving object did not hit you at a precise point in the left rib cage. How am I supposed to communicate the order for your friend's release?"

"No one would have risked getting blood on your shirt, Samuels. You are going to take me to her."

"What good will that do?"

"It means you will have to kill us both."

"And that complicates things, does it?"

"Yes."

"I fail to see how."

He said this as if the difference between one and two was negligible—unless many zeros pressed against each digit. Nor, of course, did I see how. But this had to be done, I felt, or I would not see her again.

I was angry, of course. In a foreign country, what they did was one thing. Here, another. They were picking on women.

"Have you kidnapped any children lately?"

Samuels signalled to a man at another table.

"Have Juan bring the car around."

What I was doing was dangerous, of course, possibly fatal. But I wanted Samuels to think of the danger. These guys did not like it. They wanted to avoid murder if they could. They respected men and had no use for women—that was one of their fatal flaws as we used to say—but Livy knew much more than Marie. She really was in danger. I had to do something. It was not that I had to hide my knowledge of how much *she* knew, I had to do something before they found out. They could not continue to be stupid forever. They had just made a huge mistake, however. Had it been Marie—and I now realized that they could probably not have kidnapped her and gotten her down here as quickly as I had given them credit for—I would have been in trouble, trying to make precisely the right move, maybe frozen, perhaps even saying to myself that Marie knew how to handle herself and that my interference would only endanger her. That could be the truth or a fatal rationalization. My response to Samuels came from my anger at their picking on Livy. Fear can induce paralysis. Anger insists on response—not necessarily the right response, of course.

"We wised up when you went to Brussels," Samuels said, as we stood just outside the bar.

No. They wised up when I came to Florida. They must have thought Marie was just my photographer after all! The elaborate scheme that got Marie and me together in Boston had been, they realized, a mistake, but a useful mistake. It demonstrated their power. Or, perhaps they figured that I had two women and that they could use either as a hostage. I had a sudden thought—did they know about my daughter, Katherine? These bastards threatened the people you care about. They might know where Katherine was. I did not.

Then I realized that I had behaved just as they had known I would. I had made a move. They knew that I would do what I could to deflect attention to me—the noble, knightly move that they could predict. And, I had. In their eyes, that action kept me from doing anything important. Money was important. People were not, except as icons to be manipulated on their planetary chess board.

Like any soldier going into battle, I had to assume that I was not going to die. I suppose that some soldiers figure they will die—like the Union infantry pinning name tags on their uniforms for identification after one of the early battles of the Civil War. But I had to figure that this group cannot risk too much sheer murder. Bad as this country has become under the martial law of the drug war, we aren't Chile yet, or Argentina. Of course, they could kill people who did not count. Had I managed to squeeze onto the bottom of the list of people who did count? Baldwin had, as the big boys found out to their astonishment. It had cost them to get his name placed under the "Suicide" category. The fact is, though, that they would have removed me as a possible witness once I signed the statement. I was the only one who could have come close to identifying the three of them and claiming they were in one place at the same time. Wouldn't a court be suspicious of that affidavit?

No. They will throw so many affidavits at the court that mine will be lost in the pile. If anyone asks, the lawyers were taking proper precautions against unexpected testimony.

"Mr. Kane, I hold in my hand an affidavit. Do you recognize it? Is that your signature?"

Marie, of course, had been standing next to me. I would have affirmed that I had seen nothing. Was she about to say that I, the trained observer, was blind? She could try, but it would look as if her testimony had been suborned. As so often in any legal system, the sayer of truth would be branded a liar. Then they'd prosecute her. They had it all figured out.

We drove in Samuels' limo—cruised, I should say. It moved like an inboard motorboat on a level sea—through the city, past a thousand shopping malls, each dominated by a gigantic Publix, and along a thin strip lined with motels facing the Gulf. Through the tinted windows, the hot world out there looked like an old black-and-white film. I expected Ella Raines or Dana Andrews, John Garfield or Lana Turner to pause and stare at this sleek machine from another time.

I continued the conversation as if it had not been interrupted.

I learned long ago that it is better to confront possibilities—even lousy ones—than to pretend that no one means you any harm. Get it out—insist that people recognize what they are doing, instead of making you guess. Some people do mean you harm and there's no way out of that.

"You either kill us now. I have no doubt you will be able to do that and get away with it. That's a big bay out there, full of skeletons. The weakness of your organization is your unwillingness to kill people. Or—you let us go and take your chances."

I sat between Samuels and the man who had been watching us at the Bistro.

"We do not like to kill people. We are not Murder, Incorporated."

"Don't get moralistic on me, Samuels."

"The affidavit will say that you signed it free of coercion."

"Yes, it's a powerful document. I will sign and don't plan to repudiate it. I don't think it would do any good. I'd then become one of those unreliable eyewitnesses who, as it turns out, wasn't wearing his glasses at the time he saw the crooks."

"I think you will be wise enough simply to say that that is your signature on the document," Samuels said.

I thought so, too. He was telling me that I would not die that day—at least not by his order.

Finally, we turned on to a blinding lane made of crushed shells. We came to an iron gate in a high pink stucco wall. The gate swung open, apparently of its own accord, and the lane continued under palm trees, to a pink stucco house.

"This is where Al Capone used to live, isn't it?"

"He lived on the other coast," Samuels said.

Comstock appeared, to open the car door for Samuels. We crunched across the crushed shells to the huge, oaken door of the house.

The house itself was almost cold, even after the air conditioning of the car. They must think that living like a side of beef is a healthy thing to do.

Livy was in the library, to the left of the entrance hall.

She sat on a green leather chair with the stiff posture of someone trying not to look nervous.

"Larry!"

"I am here to pick you up and take you back to—to my car, Comstock."

"Of course, Mr. Kane."

"No, Comstock. Mr. Kane's rental car will be returned to the airport in Sarasota."

"Meaning?" I asked.

"You, Kane. We will take you to your hotel. Then—where do you want to go."

"My car is in Portland."

"Oregon."

"This coast."

"Right. That makes it easier. Our pilot is filing a flight plan even as we speak. Report to the General Aviation Terminal at, let us say, 1630 hours."

"Anything else?" I asked.

"One thing, Mr. Kane," Samuels said.

"I am here of my own accord," Livy said, sounding like a recorded announcement.

"Of course you are, Livy. We both know that."

"Sign here, Kane. Juan will drive you back to Sarasota," said Samuels. "Thank you both for your cooperation on this delicate issue."

"Yes, indeed," I said. "Always happy to help the authorities with their inquiries."

Samuel raised his left eyebrow, but said nothing.

I signed the paper. I noticed that it had already been notarized. Did my signature mean that Livy and I were about to start a new red tide in these once-pristine waters? I did have to sign the paper to find out.

"My best to Dorothy," I said, handing him back his gold pen.

I saw Samuels tense, but, with that superb self-control of his, he said nothing.

Juan drove us around the edge of the city and across the Selman Parkway, known as the "Leroy" in Tampa—the first name of the great linebacker after whom it is named. This time the world out there looked like the bottom of the sea as viewed from the whirring space of a diving bell. We rolled down Route 75 to the Cattleman's Drive exit in Sarasota, then across the Trail to Siesta. Livy clung to my arm most of the way, but we said nothing. Juan pretended to speak only Spanish.

I walked Livy down her driveway to the white shingled garage that led to the white shingled house overlooking the inlet. We walked down a path and out on to a wharf, palm trees rattling, the dead-fish glint of the water slipping and slopping, hours from the wind drop at twilight.

"I was so scared."

"I don't blame you. But they would not have done anything."

"Are you sure?"

"Yes."

"Tim is sailing."

"No reason why he shouldn't be."

She was suggesting that, of course, Tim would have come to save her had he not been sailing. Well, he might have tried. Then maybe they both would be dead.

"I was shopping for shoes when the two men approached me."

"You can get those shoes tomorrow, Livy. Just one word of advice. Do not let anyone know how much you know. They are still nervous."

She shivered in the heat of a Florida afternoon.

"I haven't."

"Good."

They had kidnapped her to put pressure on me—totally misreading the emotional situation. Well, Montreal, then Brussels. They were not entirely without evidence. The macho men who ran the operation had completely underestimated the women who had been involved. The world of these hombres involved trophy wives and whores. They did not know that Livy knew as much as I did about their operation and had known it for a longer time. They had figured out how I'd respond. In some atavistic way, I was like them. They knew me better than I knew myself. There was no reason to explain any of that to Livy. It might reassure her. It might frighten her.

"They think I'm an idiot," Livy said.

I laughed.

"So my best bet is to let them keep thinking so," she said. "They know that you are more than just a pretty face."

She laughed and touched my nose, where it departed radically from its patrician design.

"They've done enough to convince me to keep quiet. My amigo, Juan, awaits me"

"I'm on my way. My best to Tim. He looks like a good man. Please invite me to the wedding."

I held her close for a moment.

We were both damp again in the saturation of heat, after the airconditioning of the sepia world of the limo.

"Don't catch cold," I said.

I got a ride up the coast in a Beachjet 400A. I was feeling cocky, so I asked the pilot to let me fly right seat. He watched me trim the plane up against a slight onshore wind, let me make a call departing Jacksonville control, and walked back to the head.

I felt good about that.

As we departed Savannah Control, I said, "You've got it, skipper. Heading 10 degrees. 270 knots. Altitude angels 21. I am going back for a beer."

I opened the small fridge behind the cockpit on the left hand side of the passenger compartment and pulled out one of the frosty Heinekens. It had been a long day.

My homecoming turned out to be more eventful than I had anticipated after the quiet trip to Florida.

"Nothing much," I said to Marie. "Some debate here and there. The bad boys gave me a ride back, though."

"And the usual beautiful woman."

"She was there."

"Why'd they give you the ride?"

"I signed their paper."

"So that's that."

"That, thank God, is that. Back to normalcy, as Harding said."

"Coolidge."

"Bet?"

"I know better. Harding."

Casey had been delighted to see me, of course. I think dogs have no sense of people coming back. And sometimes they don't. Every return is a unique event in a dog's life. Casey began yowling softly and pacing back and forth from where I sat, working on a beer, to the door. He looked at me as if saying, there's something important you should know.

There was.

"Okay, Casey," I said. "Your special squirrel asking to be chased?"

Casey leaped from the open door, just as I heard a car crunch up my driveway.

A dark blue sedan stopped.

A tall woman got out and knelt to accept Casey's wild waggling greeting.

"Katy!"

I had always thought of her as Katy, so the name came blurting out.

She saw the look in my eye. The moment was fragile.

"Yes, I have a friend who calls me Katy."

I got a cool hug.

"Go in and say hi to Marie. I'll bring your bag in. The guest room—your room—is made up."

"Who says I'm staying?"
"I do."
"Bag is in the trunk. And some things I brought for Marie."

The car purred past some tennis courts—rolled clay, drying out in the noontime sun after the sprinklers, still turning a few last diamonds on and off—and onto a horseshoe curve.

Marie and I will have to come to this place, I thought.
"Do you play?"
"I did. Once. You?"
"Once. Una vez. Funny about time."
"What is?"
"It doesn't always work in our favor."
"It's neutral."
"No. At best it's whimsical. If we had met, say, five years ago . . ."
"Yes, or during several years ago that I can think of."
"But we did not," Mercedes said. "You become one of the many faces I see in one of those escalators—going up as I come down, going down as I come up."
"Yes, that is time being whimsical."
"And a moment of love passing," she said. "I wish you could come see my ranch."
"Next time," I said.
"Yes. And bring your friend."
"Marie."
"Bring Marie."

Don Alvaro had returned my call that morning.
"You say that you have something that may be helpful?"
"I think so."
"You had better bring it in person."
"Couldn't one of your people . . . ?"
"I can trust no one with anything like this, Lorenzo. No one. What airport?"
"Where are you?"

"Guadalajara."

"I haven't got my passport renewed yet."

"No problem. Just bring an identity card."

"Portland, Maine. PWM."

"Jay Ah Ta. Serosieteserosero. Manana," he said and hung up.

"Guadalajara?" Marie had asked.

"Next time," I said.

"Dangerous?"

"I don't think so. Just down and back."

But danger usually comes when you aren't looking for it. To say that you don't anticipate any emergencies is to misunderstand the nature of an emergency. Death can arrive at the very moment you think you've got it made.

I was cruising along in my ten year old Volvo just before the traffic would begin to clog what locals called "The Bermuda Triangle," a ten mile stretch from Brunswick, past Freeport and Yarmouth, on the way to Portland. The four lane highway provides odd angles at which visibility erases itself for a moment long enough to create the sensation that you have suddenly embarked along the "WRONG WAY." Access lanes encourage races with the car in the right lane who is sometimes pinned there by the car in the left lane. Fog suddenly gulps up sightlines as the road descends toward the Royal River. The highway is slippery when it rains and slick as a Mali pool table cover when even the slightest touch of ice visits the area. Cars hydroplane along the spray sent out by the windshield washers of the car in front of them. Accidents are partly the result of weather, partly the result of drivers, partly the result of a Department of Transportation that builds roads for its own pockets, as opposed to people who drive cars, and partly the result of a spooky stretch of road that must be haunted by the vengeful ghosts of the drivers of long-crumbled buggies and one-horse shays.

I was musing about these matters, listening to a CD of Ella singing a plaintive ballad, "Next Time the Dream's On Me," thinking, God, she's been dead for five years now, wondering what sort of aircraft Don Alvaro would send for me, watching the dawn begin to outline the furry hills ahead, beginning to notice shadows shift to shades of green, and carefully navigating in the right lane, but dangerously already in the air and on the way to Mexico, when a car without its lights on came blasting up behind me.

Well, he'll pass me, I thought. The normal thing to do is to normalize situations, to fit the sound into the dream you are having. I woke up.

This car was intent on driving me from the road, and the driver had picked a spot where the highway leans toward a golf course, with a big ditch between the tiny clubhouse—it had started as a driving range—and the road. No other car was near.

I was strapped in and I had a front airbag. They would not kill me, but they'd get the envelope in my attache, sitting on the seat beside me.

The driver expected me to speed up, but then I had a chance to crash into the bridge ahead when he punched me. It is an old fighter pilot's maxim that I heard from my father. When in doubt, so what the other guy does not expect.

I hit my brakes. The other guy did not want a collision. He wanted to bounce me off the road, stop, get the envelope, and take off. If anyone else was there, he'd say he was going to call the state police over at the clubhouse. He could even mime that on a cell phone, if necessary. But it wouldn't be. He hit his brakes. As he came close, so that I could see a single face in my rear view mirror, I threw my car into third and ploughed forward. The road must have been slick with morning dew. My car slewed and straightened out as I spun the steering wheel and let it go. The car behind me must have gone from a dry spot to a wet spot on that treacherous road. He swerved to the right and rolled over, trying to pull the highway with him into the ditch.

I pulled off at Route 77 in Yarmouth. I would rejoin the highway a few miles down the road. By now, morning traffic had thickened. I thought I heard a siren looping in the distance behind me.

I shook my hands to get some of the tension out of my body and breathed oxygen in against the rush of $C_9H_{13}NO_3$ that was pounding in my ears. The bastards! They think they have an abecedarian on their hands. Had they sent a follow-up car? Maybe. Could I get to the airport? Maybe. If I had another car . . . No. The available substitutes were at the airport.

What they would do would be listen to the police scanner. What they would get was single car accident on two niner five, between Freeport and Yarmouth, driver enroute Midcoast Regional, Brunswick. Did I have any choice but to gamble on their interpretation of that report? No.

The other good thing was that I was leaving from the General Aviation Terminal—once upon a time the main terminal at Portland Westbrook Municipal.

"General Aviation Terminal," I said to the driver of the Thrifty van.

"It's right across the street, sir," he said, pointing at the brick facade.

I gave him a five dollar bill.

"I need the air," I said, swinging my bag on a seat and sitting down, clutching the precious attache to my chest.

I had left my car at Thrifty. The van would take me around the airport road. I might not shake pursuit, but I would have a chance to see who was pursuing me. By this time they might know that their driver—no Curro he!—had embraced the fate they had dictated for me.

Yes, a couple of men were watching at the entrance to Delta. They looked as if they were waiting for someone. They were, of course. I hunched down, as if praying. I was, of course, wordlessly. If they had not picked up Don Alvaro's "G A T," they would have had me booked on a Cincinnati, Dallas, Guadalajara sequence and would, with all due courtesy, have removed the attache from my grasp without arousing a tremor from the local authorities, who were probably hoping for a drug bust or two that morning.

The reason for the trip and my nearly being bounced into the weeds was a chance remark I had made.

We—the three of us—were walking to MaryEllenz, an unpretentious but wonderful Italian restaurant in Bath, on Commercial Street. It has a splendid view of the waterfront, busy now with the boats of tourists and recreational fishermen.

"Look at the sun on those leaves," Marie said.

It had just rained, and the light of evening caught the trees freeing themselves of the storm, drop by golden drop.

I had just done so, and was about to ask her to do the same thing.

A small wind raised the branches for an instant to the angle of light sliding across the low buildings. The effect was of some coordination that might find analogies in music and dance, but was not capable of metaphor.

"You just reminded me of something I've forgotten," she said.

"What?"

"Can't say—feeling, a feeling of all the past suddenly flicking in my gut and saying you got to the wrong place, you got there gradually . . ."

"But you recognize it suddenly."

"Yeah."

"I know the feeling," Katy said. "It comes after that last announcement of who you are. You say, 'What?'"

"You'll say that again. Wrong place?" I asked Marie.

"No. Right place now. But that's where that feeling came from. A disjunction."

"Light and shadow," Katy said.

"Yes. And light and light," Marie said. "It says there's so much we don't know, and won't."

"And won't," Katy said.

"And will," I said.

We swapped mouthfuls of Chicken Parmesan (Marie), Zuppe di Calamari (Katy), and Sirloin Pizzaiola (me) and traded sips of the Barolo Rosso and the Santa Margherita Chardonnay.

"Why travel to London or Paris?" I asked.

"It is good," Katy said.

"And fun," Marie said.

"Fun?" I asked.

"It's like being on vacation. You look out and see the boats and the water."

"But it's where we live!" Katy said.

"That's why it's more fun in the summer," Marie said. "It's where other people want to be."

"It's too bad we don't have that picture," I said.

"Which one?" Marie asked.

"The one of the three guys in the Hotel Colon."

"I have that picture."

"You do?"

"Sure. I slipped what's his name—Comstock—an empty roll of film. I did not know it was important."

"Jesus!" I said.

"You have not been a mine of information," Marie said.

"Dad is the original chauvinist," Katy said. "Women should be seen, preferably obscene, but not told a damned thing."

"He's improved, Katy," Marie said.

Katy rolled her eyes.

"He is always leaping off to strange places to visit beautiful women," Marie said.

"They do exist," Katy said.

"I keep saying they do," I said.

"Dream on," Marie said.

I had made copies of the photograph, of course, but the negative was in my attache. Photographs could be doctored. We would have the negative certified by whoever the greatest expert in the world might be.

I did not see any elegant hoodlums lurking near the General Aviation Building.

"Pull right up as close as you can get to the door," I said to the driver of the Thrifty van.

A steward brought me eggs and bloody marys as the Hawker Horizon angled south west against a wind from the west. Still, Portland, Maine to Guadalajara, Mexico, with enough to turn around and go back again without refueling. Don Alvaro did things right!

Mercedes met me at the airport.

"Que sorpresa!" I said.

"Don Alvaro is here on business. Not bull business, unfortunately. I am going to import his line of liquors."

She pointed at me as we went into a shed.

The customs agent glanced at my driver's license and gave me a white card.

"Please return this when you leave, senor."

"We are going to El Tapatio," she said. "It's close to the airport."

I took a last survey of the people who were filing from the just-arrived American flight out to taxis and waiting cars and clenched my folder to my chest.

"I think we are safe," Mercedes said, as we slipped behind the tinted glass of an air-cooled limo.

"It's a habit," I said. "I'll break it in time."

"You might consider keeping it," she said.

We drove to an oasis built on a wedge of mountainside five thousand feet high between the airport and the city below. The towers of the Basilica of Sapopan rose above the murky buildings and were mirrored by the mountains beyond. We walked under stucco arches filled with winds of the mountains and the thick scent of flowering plants.

We had lunch—moist turkey on crisp and lightly toasted bread and a chilly chardonnay—on the patio of Don Alvaro's suite, overlooking a three-tiered fountain that emptied into a series of tile pools surrounded by a low brick wall.

The sun shifted across the grass. A woman swam laps in the pool. She climbed out, and light shimmered from her black suit. For a moment, I thought it was Marie.

"You must come here sometime," Mercedes said.

"I was just thinking that," I said.

"Let me see it, then," Don Alvaro said.

"Here is the photo, and here in this smaller envelope, is the negative."

"Ah yes, this proves that they were in the same elevator together."

He slid the photo across the table cloth to Mercedes.

"Is that all?" she asked.

"No. They claimed that they had never met. That's been the key to their defense. They have dismissed all the paper as coincidence, sometimes as the price of doing business. Compelling as it is, it does not link them. Their collusion is a logical inference, but inference will only go so far in a Spanish court. I doubt that the judges will believe that this photograph—this framed and smiling portrait of three men accused of conspiracy—is another instance of coincidence. I will have the negative authenticated, of course. Let us celebrate over brandy, Lorenzo. Then, you have a plane to catch."

"It will wait for him. Isn't that good to know!" Mercedes said. "A shame that you can't stay to watch the sunset over the city."

"He will come here again," Don Alvaro said, laughing. "I can always tell."

"Yes," she said. "So can I."

We toasted each with gigantic snifters of DonA brandy.

"My wife's name was Dona," Don Alvaro said. "Now, Mercedes, we have other business to discuss. No siesta this afternoon!"

As I climbed into the limo again, I saw a man climb into a car behind us in the circular courtyard outside the reception area. He followed us down the hairpin curves, past the tennis courts, to the gate. I turned now and then to glance at him. Olive skin, dark eyes, making no effort to hide the fact that he was following me.

Of course, if he were leaving El Tapatito at the same time that I was, he had no choice but to follow me. We turned toward the airport. He turned toward the city.

Shortly after midnight after a few beers—altitude tends to

heighten the effect of alcohol—and a thick, rare roast beef sandwich brought to me by my never-tiring steward, I lay down on the couch to rest my body. I was going home again.

Sorry, Dorothy, I thought. No guardian angel this time. I doubted that she would starve.

"Guadalajara?"

"Mission accomplished," I said. "I'll tell you about it in the morning."

Oh yes, I would tell her about Mercedes—since there was nothing to tell. I did want to visit that ranch of hers. I planned to take Marie.

"Katy in bed?"

"Yes. Don't drop fatherhood on her again."

"Don't worry. I am not one of those, when in my house, my rules, people. I can't help being her father."

"And she can't help being your daughter."

"I'll remember that," I said.

"Please meet me at The Pier. Noon."

It was a voice I had heard before. But where?

Something was still pursuing me, even here in Newport. I had come here because a documentary for which I had written a very brief narrative had been nominated for an award.

Did I have any choice? It was June, but it felt like winter as I walked down from the Viking toward Thames Street.

The rain shatters its reflection on the street. Don't walk prints itself on bones of an umbrella, the shoulders of a crow. The stones gleam at noon as if the light is gone, and they alone illuminate. A twist of tree matches a wrung-out cloud, and wind levels the storm to parallel the blind face, there underneath the wing-borne fist. A row of headstones is losing to the grass, the slide of one, rise of other, line of names erasing in the earth, the pass of darkness. I recall the mice, consigned to drown by my grandfather, swimming to the last. That, too, was summer—1969.

I had thought of picking up the bucket and flinging it into

the field on the other side of the well. I did not. Retribution was sure to come, but, greater than my grandfather's anger, was my sense that the mice were subject to some fatality over which I had no control. If I tossed them into a field, a bunch of crows would appear above them as if summoned by a wicked witch.

I shrugged my shoulders at that memory as I turned down Howard Wharf.

I shook my baseball cap and looked into the dining room, quivering in the silver reflection of the harbor. I saw a hand raised at a table overlooking the rugged lines of a Coast Guard cutter tied up at the wharf.

It was the man I had seen—heard, really—at the museum in Malaga.

"I have a beer coming for you, Senor Kane. And I took the liberty of ordering you a steak, medium rare."

Yes, the condemned man . . .

"It is because I am on tight schedule," he continued. "I am Isidro Gallego."

Spanish, as I had known, and as I would have by the slim lines of his bespoke suit and the heavy gold of the cufflinks at each sleeve, and by eyes darker than the Spanish sky must be before lightning.

He held out his hand. I shook it across the table.

"I represent people who have been interested in what you are doing."

"I'm sure you do."

"We could do little, of course . . ."

I drained most of my beer in one drag.

"I noticed."

He ignored my snideness.

"But now . . . The photograph disproves what the defense has maintained."

"I thought it might."

"And so, with expert testimony to show that the negative has not been tampered with, the compelling but circumstantial case we have built up, is confirmed . . ."

"And so?"

"I have come personally to express my gratitude."

"You're welcome."

I watched the water in the gray bay to my left turn to gold inside the circles of the second beer the waiter was pouring for me.

"You will say," Gallego said, "that we might have intervened sooner . . ."

"I don't even know who you are."

"But it does not work that way. There are no demands in the corporate world . . ."

"What now looks like a fait accompli to you now was hardly that only a week ago."

"That is true. You state it very succinctly. We could only support a fait accompli. Had we moved sooner—even when the Spanish court convened—we might have destroyed our chance."

"And the court would have done little."

"It would have done enough, Senor Kane. As it is . . ."

"As it is, you, whoever you are, take over. Right?"

"That is cynical. What I say is that, if we take over, as you put it, the money goes where it should go."

"More of it than before."

"Most of it, Mr. Kane. Most of it. Watch for the results. Only that will prove to you that you have done a good thing. You may believe that everyone in this tiny and endangered place where we try to live is caught up in . . ."

He jabbed his right hand at the shrouded harbor.

". . . this sea of greed. Some of us, Mr. Kane, many of us, have children. They have children. We are not like your amiable former President, who says, 'Of course, I won't be around.' I will leave it at that."

That, of course, had been my motive. I recognized it as he spoke his cliches. I could feel it riding in from the water out there. It was a truth that sounded too damned sentimental as it was spoken, even as it was thought. But, yes, Katherine, this has been for wherever you will be.

"Perhaps. I will never know."

"I think you will, Mr. Kane. The results will not be kept a secret."

"Nor were the previous results."

"The results we achieve will not be merely a product of pressagentry, either."

My steak arrived, a wisp of steam curling just above its juices.

"Enjoy your meal," Gallego said. "I must be on my way. Again, my thanks. Our thanks."

He stood and held out his hand. Without getting up, I shook it again.

It would cost me nothing to make Pascal's wager.

"Thank you for coming," I said.

He bowed, turned, and walked toward the mainland, down a long perspective, gray with clouds whisking against the planking of the wharf.

I had been summoned by what I had assumed was a sinister voice. Perhaps I had been. They might still be saying, remember, we can find you anywhere, anytime. It could be just a bit of ex post facto revenge, delivered in the benign guise of an unexpected steak for lunch. I would watch for whatever the results might be. The steak makes my mouth water in retrospect and another beer didn't hurt either.

I watched the cutter slide into the rain drifting back and forth across Newport Harbor.

"The bill has been paid, sir," said my waiter.

"Tip?"

"Very generous, sir."

Back in Maine in May—cherry, dogwood, rhododendron splashed out there along the roadways, but what one noticed were the different shades of green against the constant dark green of the hemlock. It was the only time of year in which the state enjoyed any sense of delicacy. That is—unless one counted the individual design of the snowflake. The problem is that they tend not to arrive as single spies and lose their uniqueness in the huddle, as we all do in time.

I seldom remember my dreams. That's the sign of a consciousness begging to be recognized as a narrow zone of meaningless activity and also evidence of a man who, like Chaucer's Man of Laws, seems to have more busyness than business. I did remember this one. My ex-wife, still angular and still attractive, was trying to put something on the luggage rack of her station wagon. I was trying to tell her that whatever it was needed to be repaired before she put it on the luggage rack. Another person came up—a man—and agreed with me. She turned and started to debate with him. "Good," I said. "You argue with *him*!" I woke up smiling and the good mood lifted in me throughout the day.

I had filed my report and forgotten all about it, hoping I, too, had been forgotten.

I did not feel pursued any more, and I knew that the sense of nothing at my back was not just false confidence. Oh, yes—time's winged chariot, but that was a metaphor for the time being. Even the big GLOP letterhead on the envelope did not cause me to tremble. My name looked out through the cellophane from what looked like a check. Did it say "This is NOT a check"? No. A note said, "We feel that you have done an exceptional job with this report. We have added a bonus to the agreed-upon amount."

$75 000.

Blood money. Money stolen from peasants, from people dying in a race between hunger and some other disease, a vapor of cash from atop the great pool that greedy men had built up as a private reservoir on a parched planet. The money stank.

$75 000.

"Marie!"

She looked up from her *Redbook*.

"I've reached a decision."

"Let me think about it."

"How do you know what my decision is."

"I'll bite."

"Let's get married."

"I said, let me think about it," she said, returning to her magazine.

"I'll accept that as a 'yes,'" I said.

She wrinkled her face—perhaps at something she was reading.

Casey came prancing in from the kitchen and smiled at us. Katy followed with a can of Heineken in her hand.

"Can I be flower girl?" Katy asked.

fin